DAN *and the*

CAVERNS

of BONE

First published 2013 by
A & C Black, an imprint of Bloomsbury Publishing Plc
50 Bedford Square, London, WC1B 3DP

www.bloomsbury.com

ISBN 978-1-4081-7816-4

A CIP catalogue for this book is available from the British Library.

Printed and bound by CPI Group (UK) Ltd, Croydon CR0 4YY

1 3 5 7 9 10 8 6 4 2

DAN *and the* CAVERNS *of* BONE

THOMAS TAYLOR

A & C BLACK
AN IMPRINT OF BLOOMSBURY
LONDON NEW DELHI NEW YORK SYDNEY

Pour Rose et Hubert

CONTENTS

I

PARIS OR BUST
(...OR MAYBE JUST BUST)

I'm that kid, remember? The one who sees dead people?

Hey, don't freak out – it's cool! Okay, it's also pretty spooky, I know, but I've had the whole 'unquiet grave' thing sussed for years, ever since Simon came along.

Who's Simon? Well, he's like my shadow, or my ghostly guardian if you like, though if he's an angel, he's a pretty shabby one. While you're chatting to me, he's the one you *can't* see, lingering just behind your head in a veil of eighteenth-century ectoplasm, watching your every move, ready to strike.

Or gazing at the flowers. With Si, it could go either way.

Point is, though, Si's one of them – a dead person, I mean. He's the sidekick only I can see, my partner in crime. I'm the talent, he thinks he's the brains, and together we're pretty damned awesome. In a skin-of-my-teeth kinda way.

'Daniel.'

'Wait a mo, Si. I'm just getting to it.'

The thing about my line of work, though, is it's dead exhausting. I mean, here I am having to go to school every day and keep my eyes open and pretend to be normal, when every midnight – POP! – there's another one of *them* in my room, wailing about how they died too soon, moaning for my help. What's a psychic kid got to do to get a bit of feet-up time these days?

'Daniel, I must insist…'

'Stick your pony tail in it, Si, I'm getting there.'

Anyway, when I heard about the school trip to Paris, the first thing I thought of wasn't 'sacre bleu' or 'ooh la la', or even 'brunettes' (honest!). Nah, all I could see was the chance for a bit of a holiday. Some down time from all the phantom freakery that follows me about London. 'See ya in a week, Si' – that kind of thing.

But Simon was all, 'Ah, Paris, the City of Light!' and even passport control at St Pancras Station couldn't stop him from coming too. So here I am, wearing my trademark purple sunglasses and death's head coat, waiting to board the Eurostar to Paris with Si still wittering on in my ear. Because, as ever, there's a problem.

'Daniel, I simply must ask you one last time.' Si's hopping from one foot to the other – never a good sign.

'Just give it a rest, Si. You'll be fine,' I mumble. I can't speak too loudly now because some of the other kids have shuffled closer. They didn't want to, I can see that. No one ever wants to get too close to the weirdo who talks to himself, but the platform's filling up and there's nowhere else to go. I see in their eyes that they're all hoping someone else will have to sit next to me on the train.

'T'is just…' Si says, '… is it really necessary to ride the locomotive? Could we not sail? T'is said this Eurostar contrivance conveys one deep beneath the earth, through some manner of tunnel. That sounds most disagreeable.'

I slap my face into my hands. He's only scared of travelling on the train. I mean, he's a ghost for crying out loud! What's the worst that could happen? You see the kind of thing I have to deal with?

'Don't look at me like that,' says Si. He's embarrassed, I can tell, because the ectoplasm leaking from the bullet hole in his head is dribbling down like poo from a squeezed nappy.

'You don't know what it's like to be buried, Daniel. The bowels of the earth are no place for the living.'

'But you're *dead*,' I say for about the hundredth time, though I immediately regret it because a couple of nearby girls exchange looks and then edge away. Something tells me I won't be making any friends on this trip.

'I am sure we would have a more diverting time without your classmates,' Si goes on, 'and I would show you a Paris your school master couldn't even dream of.'

'Si, you just don't get how school trips work,

do you?' I more-or-less whisper. 'I have to go with everyone else, and I have to go on the train. If it's such a problem for you, don't come. Take the week off! Go powder your wig or something.'

'*Est-ce que tu vas faire ça toute la semaine?*' says a voice, and I rotate on my heel. Slowly. Our French teacher, Mr Phelps, is right behind me, and I just know he's been earwigging in on my one-sided conversation. But why's he got to talk to me in French? That's just sticking the boot in, that is.

'Er...' I say, trying to make the 'r' sound all Gallic. 'E-rrrr...'

Frenchy Phelps fixes me with his beady eye.

'I'm watching you, Dyer. And I'm sick of seeing your name at the bottom of my class, especially when you get straight A's in everything else. Why do I get the feeling there's something a bit fishy about that?'

'Je ne say pah what you mean, sir,' I say. Well, at least I'm trying.

'Don't get smart with me, boy. You may have your classmates rattled with this talking-to-someone-who-isn't-there act, but you don't impress me. If I don't see some improvement in your French by the end of the week, I'll squeeze you with extra homework until I do. Is that clear?'

'Yes, sir,' I say, 'I mean *oui*, sir.'

Typical! I'm rubbish at French, and he takes it personally. But it's not like I'm trying to wind him up – I really *am* rubbish at the old *parlez-vous*. It gets my tongue in a tangle just thinking about all those *kilos de pommes* I have to pretend to order. With Phelps on my case and Simon in a flap, this trip to Paris is looking less like a holiday by the minute.

2

'THIS EUROSTAR
CONTRIVANCE'

When we finally get on the train, I have to slide past a girl called Tanya to get to my window seat. Her face is a picture when she realizes she's drawn the short straw. But that's nothing compared to how she looks when Si settles down next to me, *in the same seat as Tanya*!

She can't see him of course, but some part of her must sense his presence, 'cause within twenty seconds she's gone green and is running to throw up in the toilets.

'Talk about invading someone's personal space,' I say. 'Can't you be more careful?'

'I apologise, Daniel.' Si arranges his frills and ponytail. 'But I thought you liked to be alone.' And he smiles his skeletal smile.

I give him the eye and say nothing. Yeah, I just love not fitting in and never having anyone who isn't dead to talk to.

The two seats opposite me – across the table – are booked for the school trip too, but no one turns up to claim them. I look down the aisle and see two kids sitting on their suitcases at the end of the carriage. Business as usual then, as we ease out of the station.

So it's a bit of a surprise when, after five minutes, someone *does* come and sit opposite me after all.

'Brian, isn't it?' I say, thinking I might as well pretend to be sociable with the freckled, rabbit-eyed kid who's suddenly there. 'Come for a bit of quiet time in the spooky seats, have you?'

Brian jumps when I speak. He's one seriously freaked-out kid, but surely I'm not *that* bad. But then I clock what's going on. Baz, the class gorilla, is eyeing up Brian from a few seats away. And now I see why Bri's come to sit near me. Even Baz keeps away from the kid who talks to himself.

Mostly.

'*Brain* Cabbidge!' shouts Baz from the safety of his seat, and laughter ripples round the train.

Brian shrinks down into the corner and hides his head in his hands. That's his actual name, you see: Cabbidge. He's good at maths too, the poor kid.

And I thought *I* had problems.

A ball of scrunched-up paper flies over and lands on the table. I think for a moment it's a bit lame of Baz to be chucking paper pellets, but then I realize what it is: a screwed-up paper aeroplane. And I remember that paper planes are Brian's obsession.

'Yeah, that flies!' shouts Baz. 'You little *freak*!'

Brian picks up the ruined plane, and, even screwed up, I can see it was fantastically complicated. But no good ever came of being clever around Baz – Brian should know that by now. He gives me a wretched look for a moment, then buries his head in his hands again. His shoulders heave, and I think I hear a sob.

Fancy paper engineering *and* a tendency to cry? I really wouldn't want to be in Brian's shoes now Baz has him on his radar. I give Si a glance, but Si doesn't return it. He's too busy glaring at Baz. Ectoplasm is puffing out of his head like smoke from a steam engine, and I see I'm in for trouble of my own if I don't rein him in.

'Easy, Si,' I whisper. 'Let's not get involved, yeah? Baz's all mouth and no trousers.'

'Trousers? Zooks, Daniel! This poor child is being persecuted – '

'Yeah, bullies do that,' I interrupt. 'But we're on holiday, remember? Baz's just a big wuss in Wookie's clothing, that's all. He wouldn't dare come over here.'

And that's when Baz comes over here.

He looms over our table, all zits and bumfluff on a stack of un-earned muscle. What was Mother Nature thinking of?

'Did you just call me a wuss, spooky boy?' Baz says to me, and I find it's gone very dark in my corner.

I let my purple sunglasses fall back down over my eyes, and hope that looking mysterious will have its usual effect.

It doesn't.

Baz carefully removes my specs, puts them on the floor, and stamps on them.

I notice that Frenchy Phelps is suddenly very engrossed in the Eurostar magazine.

'And as for you, *Brain* Cabbidge...' Baz clips poor Bri round the head, 'your sorry hide is mine this trip. If you don't do my maths homework for the rest of the year, there's gonna be grilled Cabbidge *en croûte* for breakfast. Every. Single. Day.' He raps Bri on the noggin to emphasis each full stop. 'Get it?'

Brian whimpers, and tries to shrink even further. Oh, he gets it, all right.

And that's when I decide I've had enough.

I look round at Si, and give him my *now*-we-can-get-involved look. Si's been quivering like a dainty firework waiting to go off anyway, and he leaps from his seat in fury, filling the space above us like an elderly angel of justice.

What a shame only I can see that.

Now you might be wondering what exactly he can do, what with him being just a ghost and all, but Si's got a little trick up his frilly sleeve. Telekinesis is a fancy word, I know, but there's no other that fits. Yup, you've guessed it – Si can move things with his mind.

Well, small things anyway.

Like a button, for example. And a belt buckle. Just like he's doing now.

Then, in front of everyone, I snap my fingers.

This isn't just for show, it's Si's cue to go in for the kill. Using more of his spook powers, he yanks Baz's secretly undone jeans downwards, letting them settle round his ankles. As far as everyone else is concerned though, the class bully's trousers have just fallen down all on their own, at my magical command.

There's a moment of stunned silence in the carriage. Then there's an explosion of laughter. Baz is frozen to the spot – it's a full five seconds before he shouts, 'What the…?' and begins scrabbling to hide his embarrassment.

And his Ben 10 boxers.

He shuffles back to his seat in panic, still struggling to get his jeans back above his knees. And that's when he nearly knocks over a speechless women in a Eurostar uniform, who was just coming down the aisle.

Well, Frenchy has to put the magazine down now, doesn't he, as the woman finds her voice – a French one, as it happens – and proceeds to lecture him on class discipline and the rules of travel and such. All the time Baz is cringing in his seat, and we can all hear the tinkle of metal as he tries to do his belt up again.

Simon settles back in the seat beside me with an aura of ghostly satisfaction. And, yeah, it is a triumph of sorts. I doubt we'll be bothered by Baz again in a hurry. Nice one, Si!

Brian Cabbidge stares at me for a long time It's like being studied by a neurotic squirrel. Then he bends down, scoops up the remains of my purple specs and puts them on the table in front of me like an offering. I'm not sure what to say, so I don't say anything, but I have a horrible feeling I don't need to. It feels like something's just been agreed between us.

After a while Brian gives me a nervous smile and then fishes a pad of fancy paper out of his bag. In a moment he's pulled out a sheet and is folding it, twisting and pleating as a complex paper aircraft begins to take shape between his fingers. No one dares interrupt him now, and a look of bliss settles on his face.

I glance at Si and he glances back.

'It would appear you have a *protégé*, Daniel,' says Si.

'Oi, easy with the French,' I mumble. But it's hard to escape the conclusion that Brian is now under my protection. That's all I need. I fold my arms, lean back, and try to enjoy the view out the window.

The train enters the Channel Tunnel.

3

HOTEL CAFARDS

When we get to Paris – or 'Paree', as Simon says it – a wheezy old bus picks us up at Gare du Nord and whisks us in cut-price school-trip style to our hotel. As we gaze out of the window, we see the wonders and delights of the centre of Paris spread before us like French Fancies on a tea tray –

– only to see them all vanish again as we enter the dark and dodgy streets where our hotel is. When we see the hotel, it's the girls who make the most fuss.

'Aw, sir!' comes the chorus. 'We're not staying in that dump, are we?'

'Be quiet!' Frenchy snaps, his normal charming self. 'Hotel Cafards is actually very well placed for exploring the city.'

Looking up at the crumbling, leaning façade, I'm thinking it's mostly just well placed for falling down. We were expecting something flashier, what with this being Paris and all.

As I get up to leave the bus, I spot someone in the shadow of the door of the neighbouring building. A girl in black, with a braid of bleached blonde hair over one shoulder. She flashes a pair of stunning eyes at me before vanishing inside, leaving me feeling a bit on the tingly side. But then Brian pokes me in the back, reminding me I'm blocking the aisle, so I stroll off the bus like nothing's happened.

In the hotel, Frenchy Phelps skips to reception to check us in – making the most of his first big chance to show off his grasp of the lingo with the natives. I guess he's still a bit miffed at being shouted at by that French woman on the train. But as he speaks, rolling his Rs and waving his hands like a rerun of Inspector Clouseau, the receptionist seems more interested in her newspaper sudoku. She doesn't look up at all until he has stammered to a halt.

'It iz not nececelery to make thiz str-r-range noise,' says the woman. 'I speeek Ingleesh.' And she hands over several sets of keys.

Behind her, a tall and morose porter with scarily long hands glares darkly from beneath a single eyebrow.

'We do not toler-r-rate noises at ze 'Otel Cafards,' the woman goes on. 'You will at all times be silent. Your *childr-r-ren* will be silent!'

One end of the porter's Frankenstein monobrow raises in our direction and we all take a step back.

'Oh, er, *merci*!' Frenchy manages. 'I see. But, er…' He cocks his head as if listening. '…isn't that music I can hear? Loud music?' And sure enough, we can all hear a steady *thump thump thump* from somewhere.

The woman slaps down her newspaper as if squashing a spider. She glares at Frenchy like he's next.

'It iz not *us* making zis noise, it iz not 'Otel Cafards! It iz…' and she pauses, before saying

'...*next door*,' in exactly the same voice a strawberry farmer uses when he says the word *slug*.

Frenchy, despite being a grade A dufus, knows when to back away, and he backs away now, waggling the keys and smiling with his teeth only. The woman subsides into her sudoku again, like a disappointed lobster returning to its rock. But the tall and dismal porter never takes his eyes off us as we retreat. We'll be carrying our own bags then.

'Now, listen,' Frenchy says, as we reach the bottom of the stairs. 'It's four to a room, I'm afraid...' *loud groaning* '... now, now, settle down. You'll just have to get together in groups. There is one small extra room for just two though, and I think we all know who's getting that. Dan, here's your key.'

'I'll be your room mate!' squeaks Brian.

'That's not actually necessary,' says Frenchy, as surprised as everyone else that someone is volunteering. 'There's enough space in the other rooms.'

'Yeah, he can share with me, sir,' says Baz, breathing noisily through his mouth and cracking his knuckles.

I give Baz the eye. It looks like his humiliation on the train is already wearing off, but then, I suppose that's the advantage of having the brains of a goldfish. Whatever, though – I'm missing my purple specs, and I'm not inclined to let the likes of Baz have their way. I'd love to have a room to myself, but I decide to do the decent thing.

'S'okay, Bri,' I say. 'You stick with me.'

Baz narrows his piggy eyes at me. I present him with the back of my head.

As we all make our way up the creaking, greasy stairs to the cheap rooms on the attic floor, Simon swoops about approvingly.

'I'm very pleased you have decided to take on a case while we're away, Daniel. The poor boy needs a friend.'

'I only do ghosts, remember?' I whisper. 'I don't mind standing up for him, but Bri's *not* my client.'

But then I can't help thinking about that. You see, if there's one thing I've learnt from helping the dead, it's that it would have been much better if someone had helped them out when they were still alive. I mean, I'm not saying Brian will actually do anything desperate, but with someone as sensitive and picked-on as he is, you never know. So maybe Si's got a point. Maybe I *am* on the case. And if he's sharing my room, at least I can keep an eye on him.

But when I see the room, I think I'll be keeping more than just my eyes on him: it's tiny!

Bri doesn't mind, though. He's just glad to get in there and shut a door between him and Baz.

Our room is higher up than all the others, at the top of a creaking iron spiral staircase. It's actually in a turret of some kind, and gives a view out over Paris in all directions, across a jumble of rooftops, spires and domes.

And suddenly I get a glimpse of what it is people mean when they rave about the place – the view is stunning.

'La belle Paree!' declares Simon in a torrent of ectoplasmic curlicues.

Then something brushes past me, and I turn to see Bri squeezing onto one of the dinky fold-down beds. In a moment he's got his pad out and is at his planes again. I sigh, but only so I don't say something rude. Instead, I open the window and climb out onto the roof of the hotel.

The sky above is leaden, but the setting sun pours beneath the cloud, picking out chimneys and the gold of monuments. I sit on a crooked stone gargoyle and inhale deeply, tasting the bready kitchen fumes and ripe carbon monoxide of 'la belle Paree', and for the first time, I'm daring to think this might turn out to be a holiday after all.

And that's when I notice I'm not alone.

There's someone on the roof of the building next door – a black-clad figure, with bleached blonde hair. Yup, you've guessed it – it's the girl, the one with the knock-me-sideways eyes I saw in the street below. We look at each other for a moment, before she calls out to me.

'*Bonjour.*'

Oh, great!

'Er... bon jewer?' I say, and try not to touch my hair. I'm using the grin for all it's worth. Don't get me wrong, I like girls – really like them, actually – but, well, they're *girls*, aren't they? Complicated. And this one's French!

'You are English?' she says, with a lovely accent, and I'm thinking my James Bond moment is already over, if it had even begun.

'Wee. I mean, yes,' I say. Then I add, 'School trip,' which is probably just about the dumbest thing I could say. But the way this girl looks at me with her big dark eyes makes it hard to think straight. So then I just take a deep breath, tell her my name and wait to see what happens next.

What happens next is she jumps over onto my roof and sits down next to me. She really is dressed mostly in black, with a line of accessories that pretty much covers the entire blackness spectrum, especially against the shock of her white-blonde hair. Her nails are like beetle backs, her lips are smoked rosebuds, and her eyes... well, they'd give even Edward Scissorhands something uncomfortable to think about.

'*Salut*, Dan,' she says, holding out her hand. 'My name is Lucifane.'

'*Bonjour*, Lucifane,' I say. 'Er... is that your real name?'

She turns the eyes on me, full beam.

'Are you staying in the hotel, Dan? If yes, then we will be neighbours for a while. So, maybe we will also be friends?'

I somehow manage to nod and keep the grin in place at the same time.

'But I wonder if new friends should tell all of their secrets so quickly.' And she looks away across the rooftops. 'What do you think, Dan?'

Oka-a-ay. I glance over at Si and see that he's as baffled as I am. But, since being confused by girls is one of the things I do best, I just look out across Paris too, and wait for Lucifane to do something else. A paper aeroplane shoots out of the window behind us and loops the loop, before gliding away into the evening sky. Brian's keeping busy then.

'And I do 'ave a secret, Dan,' says Luci eventually, and I guess that keeping quiet was the right thing to do after all. She looks back at me. 'One that maybe I can only tell a stranger.'

I return the look as best I can and arrange my eyebrows into the '?' position. Even Si drifts in a little closer to hear what she's about to say.

I'm almost at melting point when she finally lowers her eyes. Then she leans in close till she's breathing right into my ear and tells me in a whisper:

'...*I see dead people.*'

4

SQUATTERS' RITES

Now, I know what you're thinking, 'cause as Lucifane gets up and darts back to her own roof – leaving her bombshell still ringing in my ears – I'm thinking it too. Is she for real? Si's almost as surprised as I am.

'Zooks, Daniel!'

'Do you think she could actually *see* you?' I ask my ghostly side-kick. To my knowledge no one but me has ever seen Simon. Well, not since he lost the duel that ended with a musket ball through his brain the best part of three hundred years ago, that is.

'I didn't notice her looking, I admit,' says Si, 'but we always knew there must be others who can do what you do, somewhere.'

I shudder. It's suddenly a bit cold.

'What is it about me that attracts the strange people, Si?'

'I couldn't possibly comment, Master Dyer,' says Si, from behind a cloud of swirling ectoplasm.

I get up and adjust the coat. It's getting dark, and almost time to eat. Another paper plane shoots from the window and soars into the sky, black like a bat against the setting sun. Time to collect Brian and head down to the hotel restaurant, to see if it's true what they say about French cooking.

And it turns out it isn't. At least, not at the Hotel Cafards.

I mean, do they eat caterpillars in France? Maybe not, but the gloop they scoop onto our plates could be anything. Anything, that is, except the haute cuisine we'd hoped for. And once again, it's the girls who make the most fuss.

But as I sit there, with Bri slurping it up beside me, it's not the food I'm thinking of – it's Lucifane.

'Tis a fabulous thing, is it not?' says Si, as I push my spoon around. Sometimes it's like he can read my mind.

'Is it?' I mumble back. 'I don't know, Si. After all this time… well, it's *my* thing, the dead people thing. I'm not actually sure I'm ready to share it.'

'Zounds, Daniel! No one should be alone in this world, least of all you.' And when I don't respond, he adds with a spectral sigh, 'We should at least try to find out more. After all, the young lady is only next door.'

When the slop's finished, we have a chance to visit the town before we turn in, so the whole school group troops out of the hotel behind Frenchy. Naturally, now we're in Paris proper, he's changed into a black polo neck and beret, and he's embarrassingly eager to *bonsoir* everyone we pass.

We're staying in what is known as the Latin Quarter, though quite what's so Latin about it beats me. It's a bit rubbish actually, and chock full of tourists shouting at each other outside crowded cafés. And Simon's right about Lucifane – I *have* to find out more. I make an excuse, give Brian the slip, and dodge back to the hotel.

Back in my room I climb straight out the window and look over to the roof of Luci's place. There's no one there now, and it's getting dark.

I jump across.

It doesn't take me long to find a skylight and ladder down into the building below, where I can hear a steady throb of music. I look both ways, give Si the thumbs up, and slide down.

The music grows and thuds, and the rhythm surrounds me as I creep down a wide stone staircase with curly ironwork. Si says nothing – sometimes he knows not to bother. I'm trespassing, of course I am, but somehow the whole 'I see dead people' thing from earlier feels like an invitation. And the signs get even better when I reach the next flight of stairs, 'cause there's something sitting there on the top step, grinning at me.

It's a human skull.

With a lit candle flickering on top of it.

And there are more, one every few steps, lighting

the way down into the boom and jangle of what sounds like a party on the floor below. I pick up something from the floor. It appears to be a human finger bone.

'This ain't no dog biscuit,' I say to Si.

'Zooks!' Simon says, his ectoplasm going very small as sudden doubt crosses his face. 'Could *this* be what Lucifane meant about seeing dead people?'

I say nothing. Well, there's only one way to find out, isn't there? I put the bone on the banister, adjust my lapels and stroll downstairs into a room full of dancing and sound.

There are kids everywhere, mostly my own age or thereabouts, and what with all the styled hair and guy-liner, and the uncertain candle light, I can hardly tell who's a boy and who's a girl. Not that it really matters. I'm looking for one person in particular, and I'd know her anywhere.

And I don't have to look for long because there she is – Lucifane – lying on the back of an enormous sofa like a midnight panther waiting for her prey. Those oh-so-familiar eyes flash in the smoke and flicker, and she gives me a lazy wave. I wave back, and sense Si twitching beside me as he tries to work out if she can see him or not.

As she uncurls herself and makes her way over, I look around, take in the view. It's pretty awesome. There are skull candles everywhere, which somehow makes the dancing seem all the livelier, and maybe that's the point. The atmosphere is thick with shadows, attitude, and – is that incense? The music's great too, though I've never heard it before. And then I see something that really makes the eyebrows shoot up.

On the arm of an ornate antique chair beside me is a pair of purple shades! Just lying there, like it was meant to be or something. And there's a kid sitting in the chair, with half a dozen other pairs of coloured specs on his forehead, and more poking out of his pockets and round about. He sees me looking at the purple ones, and maybe it's the surprise on my face, I don't know, but he snaps his fingers and points at them.

'He is saying you can 'ave them.' Lucifane is at my side, though she has to shout to make herself heard. 'He sells them to tourists. Take them – no one buys them anyway.'

I put the glasses on and the world goes purple, just the way I like it. I nod at the kid in the chair. He shrugs.

35

Then Lucifane is walking out of the room and I'm following her. We head down some more stairs, the music becoming a dull throb as we leave it behind. At the bottom is an enormous pillared hallway, with a chandelier like a floating iceberg, though it probably doesn't work. Everything is in darkness here, and Luci passes me a skull candle. She lights one for herself and walks on, leaving me standing there like Hamlet.

'Daniel, what is this place?' Simon says.

'Squat,' I whisper in reply, the realisation suddenly hitting me. But, as ever, Si's still a century or two behind me.

'Squat? Why should I wish to squat, Daniel?'

I ignore him. Lucifane has turned in the doorway of an enormous marble and gold tap kitchen and is looking at me. Right now, Si's going to have to increase his vocabulary on his own.

But just as I'm about to follow her in, I stop and look back down the hall. At the end of it is an ancient wooden door, a door that is not only bolted, but – the flickering candlelight shows – actually barricaded shut with a mass of antique furniture, bin bags and junk.

'What's that?' I say.

'The cellar,' Lucifane replies, with an undecipherable look at the sealed door. Then she goes into the kitchen.

'Oka-a-ay,' I say. 'You don't want people in the cellar. But… why pile stuff against the door?'

'Indeed,' murmurs Si, at my side. 'It is almost as if they want to keep something *out*.'

Luci ignores the question.

'We only 'ave herbal tea,' she says instead, as she plugs a kettle into an extension lead that runs in through an open window. Somehow I just know it's plugged into some forgotten socket in the hotel next door. Then she lights more candles, in jam jars this time, making shadows dance round the grotesquely fabulous luxury kitchen.

'I never drink anything else,' I lie. 'Nice place you've got here.'

'It is criminal for a house this size to be left empty,' she says, slightly defensively. 'So, we 'ave made it our refuge. A place for those who are different, who feel out of place. In English you have a word for what we 'ave turned this building into, a word we do not 'ave in French.'

'Squat?' I suggest, hoping Si is taking notes.

'Yes, but...' says Luci as she pours boiling water

into two cups, filling the room with a spicy tang. She hands one to me. 'The word I am thinking of is "home".'

Oh.

I won't lie – at that moment, with Luci beside me and the whole freaking awesomeness of the party upstairs, I actually wonder what would happen if I just stayed here and didn't go back to the hotel at all. Or even London! After all, I practically *own* 'being different' and 'feeling out of place'.

But I pull myself together as Si coughs politely behind me. Before anything else happens, I have to get something straight.

'I've never met anyone like you before,' I say to Luci, but then, when that makes her start doing the eye thing again, I add quickly, 'No, I mean, what you said earlier? About seeing dead people? Because, well… I'm the same. I see dead people too. Been doing it for years, got the doctor's notes and everything.' And then I jab my thumb at my spooky sidekick. 'Luci, meet Simon.'

Si steps clear into the candlelight then, and does his lowest and frilliest bow. The ectoplasm streaming from the hole in his head billows around, making him look like an eighteenth-century painting in a Baroque picture frame. It's quite a show.

'*Enchanté, mademoiselle,*' he croons.

And that's when I notice we aren't alone in the kitchen.

Someone is standing in the corner furthest from the candles, and I can tell immediately it's one of them. A dead person, I mean – a ghost. And this one is so wet-looking that it doesn't take a genius to work out how he died. The ectoplasm pours off him like the water he obviously drowned in. He's a kid about Luci's age, but his face is a blank of anguish and despair between straight curtains of sodden spectral hair.

'Is that one yours?' I say to Lucifane, pointing at the teen spirit in the corner. Then I notice she still hasn't responded to Si. In fact, she's not looking at Si at all, just straight at me. And the look is getting darker by the second.

'Er…' I say, pointing to the ghost in the corner again. 'Um…?'

'Is it normal in England for new friends to laugh at each other?' Luci says in a voice like ice, and I go 'er' and 'um' again, because frankly I don't know what's going on now. I look at Si for help, but he's already swooped over to the other ghost. He's back in a few seconds though, raising his arms helplessly.

'He is one of the newly dead, Daniel, and still in a state of shock. The only thing I could get out of him were the words "Jojo la Mouche". Their name is often the only thing the dead can say in the days just after decease, but that would be a strange name indeed.'

I look back at Lucifane, and now I see her eyes are glistening. There are actual tears there, and girls + tears = warning bells in my experience. I need to stop going 'um' and try to think of something more coherent to say. But all I can manage is…

'Luci, who is Jojo la Mouche?'

The kitchen is filled with the sound of shattering china as Lucifane's teacup hits the tiles. Then my ears almost explode as her scream erupts, and Luci – the panther all over again – jumps at me.

Oh, crapsticks!

I don't hang around to feel those fingernails.

5

'WHAT IS IT, THAT IT IS?'

When I climb back in through the hotel window, I'm breathing so heavily I'm lucky not to wake Brian. Well, so would you be too if you'd just run up four flights of stairs with a horde of angry French Goths on your tail.

'What in Death's name just happened, Si?' I gasp. The teacup – amazingly still in my hand – is rattling wildly in its saucer. 'She couldn't see him, could she? She couldn't see *you*!'

'I fear we may have misunderstood the situation, Daniel.'

'Misunderstood? When someone says they can "see dead people", that sounds pretty clear to me!'

'Ah, but only because you actually *can*.' Si's got his annoying I've-worked-it-all-out-now face on. 'Consider it from Lucifane's point of view. She was trying to tell you something, but never expected you to take what she said literally.'

'Okay, Einstein's Grandad,' I forget to whisper. 'What *was* she trying to tell me, then?'

Brian rolls over and stretches. I hold my breath and put the teacup down. I could do without him waking up and asking where I've been.

'Daniel,' Si continues, 'something terrible has happened next door, in the squit...'

'Squat, Si, it's a *squat*! The last thing I need right now is a squit.'

'Very well, something terrible has happened in the *squat*. Somebody has recently died and his spirit is trapped, unable to pass on to the Hereafter. That someone – Jojo la Mouche – needs our help, and Lucifane clearly needs it too.'

'Now stop right there, Si. I've got enough on with babysitting Brian here. I don't need another job.'

But Si's giving me that mega-arched-eyebrow look only someone in eighteenth-century makeup can pull off. He knows I'm burning to find out what's going on next door, just as he is. But I'm not in the mood to give in to him right now. So when he opens his mouth again...

'Daniel?'

...I roll away into my blanket, fully clothed.

'Just buzz off, Si. Go and bother a badger. I need to think.'

And I've got a lot to think about: the palatial squat with its cooler than ice-cream kids, the cellar door barricaded on the outside (what is *that* all about?), the candle skulls (again, *huh*?), the teenage ghost in the kitchen...

Lucifane.

Yeah, it's a long time before I get to sleep.

The next day, as we risk our teeth on the bullet-hard breakfast croissants served at the Hotel Cafards,

Frenchy Phelps goes over the programme for the day. And if I'd thought I could somehow sneak back to the squat and make things right with Lucifane, then an extensive guided tour of something called 'the catacombs', followed by a written test (to make sure we were all paying attention), will put paid to that.

In no time at all, we're trooping onto the flea-bitten bus again.

'Si, what exactly are these catacombs?' I manage to ask without attracting too much attention. Bri is so close that he can't help but hear, and he looks at me with curiosity.

'A catacomb is an underground graveyard,' says Si. 'There are ossuaries and tunnels beneath Rome that are known as the catacombs, but if there is such a thing in Paris it must be from after my own time.'

'Si, "after your time" covers about two hundred and fifty years, so that's not very helpful.'

'Then I can only suggest we wait and see.' Si puffs a cloud of his more superior ectoplasm at me. 'This will be an education for us both.'

The bus gasps to a stop. Frenchy jumps to his feet and starts yelling at us to wait and settle down. He's wearing his black polo neck pullover again, but with a red waistcoat this time, and I swear, he's started growing a little goatee in his eagerness to fit in.

On the pavement, we gather before a windowless stone building with a pair of wide wooden doors. There are a few tourists milling about and blinking in the sun, and it's then that I realise that we really are going to be spending time below ground. Si seems to realise it too, and he starts quivering in his stockings again.

'Perhaps you can just tell me about it afterwards, Daniel. I'm feeling a little off colour.'

'Si, the last time you had any colour in your cheeks, it was painted on with arsenic and whiter than a vampire's bum.'

'When…' comes a little squeaky voice beside me. I'd almost forgotten Brian. '…when you talk to yourself like that, is it…? I mean, is it really…?'

'Spit it out, Bri,' I say. 'Is it because I'm loopy, is that what you're asking?'

'No, no!' he answers, just a bit too quickly. 'It's just… well, it must be weird to have an imaginary friend.'

I sigh.

'Yeah, Brian. It's a bit weird.'

'It's just, I was thinking… well, what with all this trouble with Baz and everything, I wonder if maybe, you'd… sort of…'

I sigh again. And it takes some effort, too, because my lungs are still empty from the last one.

'You'd rather I didn't talk to him? Because of Baz?'

Brian nods so vigorously I can almost hear his eyeballs rattling.

I can't believe this. But I really don't have time to argue about it, so instead, I just speak out loud to Simon, right in front of Brian and everyone.

'Okay, my weird imaginary friend, why don't you take the morning off. Go put your heels up and blow smoke rings till I get back.'

Si looks a bit surprised to be spoken to openly like this, but he's so keen to avoid going underground again that he just gives a quick bow and then vanishes in a puff of ectoplasmic relief.

I turn back to Brian.

'Is that better?'

Brian – who obviously didn't see any of that – looks a bit dubious, but nods anyway. Then he looks down at a half-finished paper plane in his hands.

'And I suppose I'd better stop making these. I'm drawing too much attention to myself.'

I look at the plane. Its design is fabulously complex. And suddenly I'm angry, though it takes a moment before I realise why.

'Brian, do you *want* to stop making your planes?'

'No, but…'

'Then don't! Baz doesn't get to decide who you are, does he? Or what you do?'

'No, but…'

'Button it, Bri. Just leave him to me and finish your plane. Something tells me today is the day we deal with Baz for good.'

'Do you really think so?'

I adjust the coat and my new purple specs. Brian looks wide-eyed for a moment, then a little smile appears and he starts folding his paper masterpiece again. But he doesn't get far. Before I can react a big beefy hand slaps down onto his shoulder. Another slaps down on mine.

'Morning, losers,' come the lumpen tones of Baz. 'Did I hear my name? Can't get enough of me, eh? Had time to think about my overdue homework, have we, *Brain* Cabbidge? Good man!' Then he clonks Bri round the head and laughs, 'Hur hur hur.'

I shrug the slab of fingers and thumb off my shoulder.

'Watch it, Baz,' I say, doing the spooky eyebrow thing for all I'm worth. 'Wouldn't want to see your jeans at half-mast again, would we?'

I'm hoping there's still a bit of protection to be had from his embarrassment on the train, but when Baz opens his denim jacket, I see that I'm out of luck on that score. He's wearing a belt *and* braces.

'I don't know how you did that yesterday, spooky boy.' Baz leans over me, so close that his bumfluff tickles my forehead. 'But try any funny business today, and you'll be seeing the rest of Paris from a wheelchair. Got it?'

And he pokes me in the chest so hard I actually sit down on the pavement.

I'm just about to see red – quite a feat for someone wearing purple specs – and get all paranormal on him again, when I remember I've sent Si off for the morning.

Crapsticks.

I get to my feet, but what can I do? Baz is about twice my weight, and he knows it. He simply grabs Brian in a headlock and walks him away, as if everything I've just said means nothing. The last I see of Brian is his helpless little ferrety face looking at me pleadingly, the plane still clutched in one hand, before he's lost in the crowd of tourists.

But as I straighten the coat and flick the lapels back up, I quietly promise Bri I won't let him down. I meant what I said: I'll find a way to stop Baz bullying him for good, with or without Si.

As for Frenchy, he's almost quivering with excitement. As he gets us to group together, I see that he's got one of the natives captive, and it's quite a specimen: a tall, hook-nosed man is standing beside him, wearing some kind of uniform. Police, it looks like, and judging by the splendour of his hat and lapels, pretty senior. Frenchy's fawning over him.

'Now class, we are incredible lucky today. *Mais oui!* For our guided tour of the catacombs, we are extremely privileged to be shown around by none other than *le Commandant* Lavache, head of the special police force charged with protecting this unique part of the city's heritage. *Quelle chance!*'

Commander Lavache turns his impressive nose on Frenchy, peers down at him along it, then turns it back to us. He looks like he'd rather be anywhere on the planet but here with a bunch of British school kids and their prancing teacher.

'Sir,' says the girl called Tanya. 'What's this catacombs, then? A shopping centre?'

There is an exaggerated gasp of horror from Frenchy. But it's *le Commandant* who speaks, and in an accent as thick as Dijon mustard.

'You ask, what is it that it is? This is really what it is that you are asking? Ignorant child! It is a monument to the glory of the dead of Paris, is what it is.'

There's a murmur round our group as everyone tries to untangle such interesting grammar, but me, I'm mostly just stuck on the mention of the dead. If I'm going to tackle Baz today, at least it sounds like I'll be doing it on home territory.

Le Commandant waves a perfectly manicured hand at the entrance to the Catacombs.

And then, whether or not we've actually understood what it is that we are about to see, we're all shuffling inside.

6

THE EMPIRE OF THE DEAD

There are steps going down. As we descend the air gets heavier and cooler, and we all go a bit quiet, not really sure what to expect. Even Frenchy clams up.

When we reach the bottom *le Commandant* tells us to walk in single file, setting off ahead of us at a military pace. I try to get nearer Baz and Brian, but the passage we're in is too narrow. The stone of the walls is white-gone-to-green and clammy, and I button the coat up. Nice place!

The corridor ends, and we find ourselves below the vaulted rock ceiling of a rectangular chamber. There is a stone doorway opposite, in an old-fashioned style that Si would probably go for if he wasn't too much of a wuss to follow me down here. Above the doorway, in curling letters of lead, is an inscription:

ARRÊTE! C'EST iCi L'EMPiRE DE LA MORT

By now we're all seriously huddled together. The girl called Tanya even clutches my arm for a moment, before realising whose arm it is and dropping it with a squeal of fright. I give her the grin, and she vanishes in an instant.

Le Commandant sweeps his nose-mounted gaze across us all before speaking.

''Ere, you are at the door to the Empire of the Dead. This is what it is saying, 'ere.' And he points to the inscription. 'I will be watching you. You touch *one* thing, you misbe'ave, and I will 'ave you strung up by the – '

'Thank you, *Commandant*!' Frenchy gasps. 'Please be assured that my class will be on its best behaviour. Perhaps, before we go in, you could give us a quick history of the catacombs? I'm sure we would all benefit from your years of wisdom as guardian of this place.'

Commander Lavache looks at Frenchy like an eagle regarding a lame rabbit it just can't be bothered to catch. There's an awkward pause as it becomes clear that the Frenchman is going to do no such thing.

Frenchy Phelps tugs his tiny goatee in desperation before filling the silence himself.

'Well, class, you see, beneath Paris is a vast network of tunnels, quarries and natural caverns. When the city graveyards became overcrowded at the end of the eighteenth century, human remains were collected together in some of these tunnels, and, well... you will see for yourselves.'

Le Commandant walks through the doorway and vanishes into the blackness. No one seems too keen to be the first one in after him, so I decide it had better be me. After all, who better to have a shufti round the Empire of the Dead than the kid who sees dead people?

But what I see when I get into the next chamber is not only an eye-opener, it also explains some of the weirder stuff that's been happening lately. Because the walls of the next chamber aren't made out of stone at all. They are made out of bones.

Human bones.

Long leg bones are arranged lengthways so that the nobbly ends are like mildewed flints in an old church wall. Only this is a wall topped not with bricks but with pelvises. Every few paces a skull stares blankly out. And where have I seen a lot of skulls recently? Yup – Luci's place. Suddenly an explanation for the blocked-up cellar door in the squat presents itself. But what can they be worried about down here? And how does it all fit in with the ghost of Jojo la Mouche?

'Sir,' I say, giving Commander Lavache the eyebrow. 'Are there other entrances to this place? I mean, do some people have private ways in, from their houses?'

The Commander stalks over and casts his eyes over me with unconcealed disdain. He reaches out and flicks his finger tips at the Tippexed skulls on my coat.

'If I 'ad my way, your type would not be allowed down 'ere. Death is not a game. But yes, there are still some unofficial ways in. We sometimes find pee-pul down 'ere oo should not be down 'ere.' Then he leans in close. 'We dee-eel with zem.'

Frenchy jumps over and starts nodding ingratiatingly.

'Yes, as I explained, class, *le Commandant* is none other than the head of the police department charged with protecting the catacombs. Trespassing is a growing problem, I understand…'

'What, people actually come down here on their own?' cries one of the girls, staring aghast into the grinning face of a skull. 'But, sir, it's horrible down here.'

'Well, some people are funny that way,' says Frenchy, and I notice him flicking a glance my way. 'There are many in Paris who enjoy these tunnels and galleries – they aren't all filled with bones. In French, these people are known as *les cataphiles* – those who love the catacombs. I believe that the police who guard them are called *les cataflics*…'

Frenchy tails off as he sees the thunderclouds gathering over the brow of *le Commandant*'s nose. If he thought he was going to impress the Frenchman with his knowledge of the lingo, he's obviously miscalculated.

'I see zat you know all about ze catacombs, Monsieur Phelps. So, I will leave you to ze rest of your vis-eet. I 'ave business to attend to. There 'as been an act of vandalism 'ere recently, and… somezing else.'

And with that he stalks off toward two policemen who are waiting in the shadows of the cavern. They snap to attention as he approaches.

'Sir, can we just say we've seen the skulls now and get out of here?' says the girl called Tanya.

'Yeah, let's quit this dump,' come the murmurs of agreement.

But Frenchy's having none of it. He starts leading us around, pointing out strange carvings here and freakish arrangements of bone there. The Empire of the Dead is well named, but I wonder what all these people would have said if they'd known in advance they'd one day end up as wallpaper in some creepy-kitsch tourist attraction.

And that's when I see him. The ghost of Jojo la Mouche, that is.

At first I'm not sure – in such a place I'm half expecting to see spirits wandering all over the place – but there's no mistake. I'd recognise that soggy ectoplasmic look anywhere. Down a dark

56

passageway that has been grilled off with rusting iron bars, the empty-eyed teenage ghost from Lucifane's kitchen drifts toward me.

'Er… hi!' I say, as he sweeps through the bars. Then I add '*Salut!*', copying the greeting I heard yesterday in the squat. He doesn't answer, he just floats down the corridor, right through a group of my classmates. I see them gasp and shiver at his passing, and then hurry away. The only thing they can see which accounts for their strange feeling is, of course, me.

Alone again, I jog after Jojo for a little longer, but he's starting to fade now. I make one last attempt to communicate, but it's no good. Simon has often explained that the newly dead take a few days to become aware of themselves again, and if Jojo isn't ready yet, there's nothing I can do about it.

Then he's gone, splashing through the wall of bones in a burst of ectoplasm only I can see.

I'm staring at the wall where he was, wondering what to make of it all, when I hear a squeak I have come to know all too well. It's coming from the next chamber. I peer round and see – in a dark corner – something both horrible and grotesque.

7

MY INNER NINJA

I t's Baz.

He's the grotesque part. What's horrible, though, is the fact that he's standing on top of Brian Cabbidge, and zooming poor Bri's paper plane around like a giant five-year-old playing with a new toy. Brian squeaks with every move of Baz's feet. Baz goes, 'hur hur hur' with every squeak.

I sigh, and for a moment I wonder about just dropping this whole business with Brian – I really don't need this, not with having to sort things out with Luci. Maybe I should just leave Brian to his fate – after all, what can *I* do against the boy mountain and his zitty biceps? I mean, I'm not exactly built for the rough stuff.

But hey, I'm the kid who sees dead people, remember? And I've learnt a thing or two from my spooky clients over the years, including some pretty nifty martial arts moves. I may not have my spectral sidekick to back me up right now – so yeah, I'm going to have to do this the old-fashioned way – but if Baz comes at me, I reckon I can get the better of him. And what Baz really needs is to be brought down a peg or two. It's almost an act of kindness.

I straighten the lapels and set the specs for action.

'Baz, I was wondering,' I ask, strolling up to him. 'Have you always looked like a monkey's bum, or does your mum do your make-up?'

Baz looks confused for a moment, his mouth falling open. The paper plane zooming slowly stops.

'I like the way she's left a little fuzz on your top lip though,' I continue, keeping my arms loose and ready. 'Girls love that. And whatever you do, don't cover up those zits either. If you took a pen and joined them all up, I reckon they'd spell "Pineapple Pizza".'

Whoosh!

The plane is flying for real now, zooming straight at my face, its paperclip tip gleaming. I drop, letting it pass over me. Then I pull the classic karate stance and start weaving about, ready to unleash my inner ninja and turn Baz's every move against him.

But there's a problem.

Baz doesn't actually throw a punch. He doesn't aim a kick or a head-butt, or do any of the things he's supposed to. He just piles straight into me like the entire New Zealand rugby team. The wind is knocked clear out of my lungs and I'm carried through the air. When we hit the wall, I can hardly see it for flying bones.

And my inner ninja? Well, I doubt there's *any* martial arts move for getting out from under half a tonne of bully.

I try to get up anyway, but all I do is free my head enough for Baz to lock his arm around it. I manage to say something, though only just:

'Crapsticks… cof!'

The sound of the collapsing wall echoes round the chamber. Absurdly, even though my nose is being pressed into the shingle, my attention is caught by something white in the air above. It's the paper plane, still looping around in the cavern.

Then there are footsteps running towards us.

In a flash, Baz leaps up. For a moment I think he's after Brian again, but then I realise it's not that. By the time Commander Lavache has burst into the chamber with the two policemen, Frenchy and the rest of my class just behind, Baz is standing innocently in a corner, pointing at me like he's shocked by the terrible mess I've made.

Lavache strides towards me as I lie in a heap of skeletal ruin, his face a mask of outrage. But before he can say anything, before *anyone* can do *anything* at all, something completely unexpected happens.

Remember Brian's plane? Well, it finally runs out of zoom and stops looping around. It levels gracefully and comes in for landing.

Right into Commander Lavache's left eye.

In any other circumstances this would be hilarious. But it looks as if even desecration of a monument to the dead is not as serious as poking a French police chief in the eye with fancy paper engineering. I swear, Lavache is almost purple with fury as he snatches the dart and looks wildly about with the other eye.

'Ooo…. ooo…?' he splutters, a vein throbbing on his forehead. 'Oo is it oo 'as done zis?'

Thing is, when it comes to paper planes, *everybody* knows oo it is oo 'as done zis.

'Brian Cabbidge!' shrieks Frenchy Phelps, who leaps forward and grabs Bri by the ear. 'You and your idiot paper folding! Look what you've done!'

Then, while Brian is still opening and shutting his mouth – no doubt in the hope that something clever will come out to save the situation – one of the policemen grabs him too, and he is marched over to Lavache. The Commander, his hand over his left eye, screws the plane into a ball. Just as Bri looks like he's finally going to speak, Lavache proceeds to demolish him with a torrent of horrible-sounding French. I get to my feet, but everyone seems to have forgotten about me in their eagerness to pour anger and derision onto poor Bri. And all the time, Baz looks on.

'Hur hur hur.'

Then the Commander announces that 'zis vis-eet is over!' and Brian is led away. Only once does he look up. He catches my eye and gives me a look of despair. Then he's gone. The rest of us are ushered out past the spilt bones in silence.

I'm about to head for the exit too, musing on how spectacularly badly my attempt to help Brian has gone, when a big beefy hand grabs me by the shoulder and spins me round.

'That was classic, that was!' says Baz. 'But before I forget…'

He reaches up, removes my new purple specs, and grinds them into the shingle floor.

'Aw, don't look so down, spooky boy,' Baz says, before I can speak. He gives me a pretend hug that knocks all the air out of my lungs once again. 'The best is yet to come, eh?'

Then he lopes off like an ogre who's late for a ballet class.

'What's that supposed to mean?' I call after him, but all I get in reply is 'hur hur hur' echoing back down the corridor. And I have no choice but to follow it.

Well, it's all about as bad as it can be for poor Bri. What was I thinking of, trying to deal with Baz with brawn instead of brain? And what exactly did Baz mean by 'the best is yet to come'. *What* best?

I've got a nervy back-of-the-mind feeling that this disaster isn't over yet, that I've missed something important.

Back upstairs, we can't leave straight away though – there's a queue at the exit. I join it and glance down the line of kids, wondering what the hold-up is. There are more policemen ahead, and beside them, on a desk, is a red velvet cushion with something on it.

It's a small pile of bones.

And everyone is having their pockets and bags searched.

'People actually steal them?' I say out loud. But then I already knew that, didn't I? How else would Luci and her friends have so many skull candle holders around? It's kind of weird, though, isn't it, stealing bones? And that's when – as I reach the head of the queue myself – I understand with a turn to the stomach what Baz meant by 'the best is yet to come'.

I try to slip back down the corridor, but it's no good. Everyone can see I'm next and there's nowhere to hide. A policeman's beckoning me over. Baz has got me good and proper this time.

The shoulders sag. I don't even wait to be searched.

I reach into my coat pocket, pull something out and hand it over.

It's an arm bone, one of the ones that got knocked to the ground when Baz torpedoed me into the wall.

And what's the French for 'I didn't put it there, Honest! It was the class bully, when he pretended to give me a hug!'?

No, I don't know either.

A gloved hand grabs me by the coat and then I'm outside at last, blinking in the sun, being marched toward Brian who is cowering beside a police van. Commander Lavache, holding a hanky over his left eye, lays off shouting at Bri when he sees me coming, but when he hears what was found in my pocket he erupts like Mount Indignant once again.

Phelps makes a pathetic attempt to intervene, but he can't get a French word in edgeways, and just sags beside us. All the while crowds of tourists look on amused, as if half-expecting the guillotine to be trundled out so that *le Commandant* can deal with us all for good.

And Baz? Well, he's at the front of the crowd, with his ape's grin all over his face.

But then I spot someone I recognise amongst the tourists and rubberneckers. It's the Sunglasses Kid, the one I saw at Lucifane's place. He's moving towards us, slipping through the crowds with his hands in his pockets, a rainbow of coloured specs dotted about him as before.

He manages to get alongside me now that the commander has turned his full fury onto Frenchy. He leans in and hands me a pair of purple specs with an expression that says 'you get through a lot of these, don't you?'.

I smile my thanks and slip the glasses on. The kid stays there, nodding, so I raise my eyebrows to ask if I'm forgiven for what happened at the squat last night.

The kid shrugs, but in such a way that I understand 'yes'. And I like this non-verbal communication – it's much better than trying to speak French. So I throw out a big fat shrug of my own, arranging my hands to ask if I'll be welcome round there again.

Something lopsided that could almost be a smile briefly appears beneath the kid's fringe. Then he points a snapping finger at me and slides back into the crowd as if he's on wheels.

I like this kid.

And by now I've completely screened out the shrieking policeman, Baz's laughter and the general rubbishness of this whole situation.

Because – if I've understood that last gesture correctly – it looks like I've got a date.

8

DEATH BY A THOUSAND CHEEKBONES

In the end it couldn't have worked out better for me. I'm in so much disgrace that I'm basically under house arrest at the hotel until we go home in a few days. And according to Frenchy, I'll be missing 'all the fun' – no Eiffel Tower, no river trip, no Louvre for me, and serve me right! But I think he's mostly just cross because his I'm-so-French routine got seriously dented by a mob of laughing tourists and a furious chief of police. I don't care though – being kept in means I'll have no trouble getting back to the squat.

It's Brian I'm worried about. He's in the dog house too, which should mean I can keep an eye on him till we get home. Only now, as we sit in the lobby of Hotel Cafards, he'll hardly talk to me at all.

'Hey, I was doing my best, Bri.'

A small, glistening eye peers out at me from under his arms.

'It's all your fault!' he squeaks. 'You said I should keep on making my planes, that I shouldn't let Baz intimidate me. But now look!'

'I didn't mean you should make one under his nose, you numpty!' I say back. 'I just meant…'

But Brian's head has vanished again. His shoulders heave.

'I'll never make another plane again,' comes the muffled voice. 'Ever! Thanks to you!'

I sigh. I really don't have time for all this now. And I can't help noticing that the hotel receptionist and that monstrous porter are staring in my direction. There's a steady thump of next door's music again, and my mind goes to Luci. I dodge out of sight, help myself to an apple and half a baguette from the dining room, and stroll back up to my room.

Where Simon is waiting.

'Well, Daniel? Did you have an eventful morning?'

'Nah.' I say, avoiding his eye. 'Cept, yeah, hold on – I saw Jojo's ghost again. Down in the catacombs.' And I give Si a quick summary of that small part of the morning's fiasco.

'Then you are right, Daniel – the barricaded door in the squat must communicate with the catacombs. T'is a pity we cannot go back and ask Lucifane some more questions.'

'Cool it, Si,' I say, taking a bite from my apple. 'As soon as the sun goes down, that's exactly what we're going to do.'

It's evening and dark again, and Si and me are creeping over the roof of the squat. I've had to wait till later than I'd wanted, but as far as I can tell the rest of my classmates are in bed now.

'Why is young Brian looking so downcast, Daniel?'

'Is he?' I say.

I see that the skylight has been left open, so I slide down the ladder before Si can ask any awkward questions. I land, once again, in the empty top floor room of the squat.

Where everything is silent.

No music, no dance noise, and so dark I can barely see in front of me. But there is a glow beyond the door. I creep forward, trying not to creak the floorboards.

At the top of the stairs, the skull I saw yesterday is still there, a newly lit candle dribbling wax into its eye sockets. I feel a bit differently about it now I know where it's come from. I tiptoe past and begin my descent.

'Are you sure about this?' Simon says, whispering though he doesn't need to. 'We didn't exactly make a good impression on Lucifane last night.'

'Si, just relax and let me handle her, yeah?'

'But...'

'But nothing. Now shush.'

More candles lead straight down to the big room where the party was. Today, there's just a strong atmosphere of incense and silent anticipation. I push the door open and pop my head round.

And there she is, sitting cross-legged in the middle of the floor, a skull candle to either side. Her dark eyes don't leave me as I edge into the room, trying not to look like I'm half ready to run, even though I am. Behind her – lounging in chairs or leaning on walls – are the rest of them, watching me too, their eyes sparkling in the candlelight. Among them is the Sunglasses Kid.

'Hey,' I say, hoping to strike a professional tone. I keep the grin switched off for now though – it might not be the moment.

'So, you come back,' says Lucifane.

'I think you need my help. Or at least, Jojo does.'

At the mention of the name, a rustle of movement and murmuring rolls round the room. One or two of the kids look ready to leap up and rush at me, but Luci lifts her hand for silence.

'How do you know about Jojo?'

'I see him,' I say. 'Well, not now, but I saw him in your kitchen yesterday, and today down in the catacombs. Like I said, I see dead people.'

The silence that follows is hostile. Lucifane stands. Then she speaks again. 'Prove it.'

I hear a click behind me, and turn to find two emo kids have swung the door shut. They fold their skinny arms. Oops.

The grin comes on automatically now, and I turn to Simon.

'Well, don't look at me,' he says. 'You're the one who can handle her, apparently.'

'Yeah,' I manage to say through clenched teeth, 'with a bit of help from my old spectral buddy, I meant.'

Lucifane steps closer, and the others do the same. Now there's a circle of hard mascara and pale cheekbones drawing tighter around me.

'Si?' I say out loud. 'Now would be a really good time, actually.'

He rolls his eyes at me.

'Maybe all you want is to laugh at us,' says Lucifane. 'But if that is why you are here...'

'I swear to you, it's true. How else would I know about Jojo?' Then, to one side, I hiss, '*Si!*'

Lucifane is close now, and it's starting to look like I'm about to suffer death by a thousand Goths. But then there's the sound of snapping fingers.

Everyone looks round at the Sunglasses Kid. He's pointing, his mouth open beneath his impenetrable fringe. It's the most emotion I've ever seen him display.

We all follow his finger.

The smoke from the incense is tumbling into the middle of the room, gathering in an entirely unnatural way. The kids back away now, agog, as the smoke cloud builds further until it becomes a misty column right in front of me. Then it fills out into the shape of a man in ragged eighteenth-century clothes.

It's Si, of course.

For a moment the smoke is so dense and carefully gathered that it forms his face perfectly, and Si smiles before giving one of his most rococo bows. I swear I can almost hear silver bells. Even the ribbon on his ponytail is visible in curling perfection.

Then the smoke puffs out in an explosion as Si lets go of it with his mind. A cloud of intense perfume hits us as the fumes roll randomly away and begin to drift into the four corners of the room, dissipating and tumbling to nothing. But now Luci and the kids of the squat are hanging back and staring in fear and astonishment at the empty space in the centre of the room.

'Nice one, Si,' I murmur to my sidekick, who floats invisibly at my side, looking unusually pleased with himself. Then I adjust the coat and say to Luci and her friends, 'Cool. Now maybe you'll tell me what's going on.'

9

GRIM DEVELOPMENTS

It takes some time to clear the rubbish and stuff from in front of the cellar door. Then there are the bolts and padlocks, all obviously added in a recent hurry. But when the door is clear, the kids hang back. Luci takes a deep breath, turns the enormous iron handle and drags the door open. Naturally, it creaks like Halloween.

Cool damp air sweeps over me. I feel it through my hair like invisible fingers. But there must be something more than creaking doors and a chill for these kids to look so scared.

'The catacombs?' I say.

Luci nods.

'But what happened to Jojo?' I ask.

'He is missing. We were all down there, when… when we saw *it*. We ran. When we got back, Jojo was not with us. We 'ave not seen him since, but… we hope.' And she turns to look down into the dark.

I glance at Si.

'You must tell her the truth,' he says. 'It is not right to let her hope.'

He's right. If Luci is waiting for Jojo to walk in through the front door one of these days, with a fresh baguette and an interesting story, she's going to be waiting forever. But that's not what's bothering me at the mo.

'*It*?' I ask instead. Well, I'm not going to let *that* pass, am I?

Lucifane steps back from the door, paler than the pale bits in a black and white movie.

'Death. Death is down there.'

'The creepy engravings and the bones and all that?'

'No, Dan – *Death*! *He* is in the catacombs, *in person*. He has driven us out.'

I can't help the grin spreading across my face.

'What, you mean, black gown, skeleton face and a scythe? Lots of teeth and no need to go on a diet? Are you serious?'

I only have to look at their faces to see that they are.

'But there's no such thing as a person called Death!' I say, and I mean it. After all, *I'd* know, wouldn't I? We'd be chums on Facebook, at least.

'I thought there was no such thing as ghosts,' says Luci, 'but we all saw that flowery man in the smoke upstairs.'

'Flowery?' gasps Si, flicking his ribbon over his shoulder. 'What can she mean, Daniel?'

But I ignore that.

'Ghosts are one thing,' I say to the whole lot of them. 'But Death? The Grim Reaper? That's bonkers!'

'Bonkers?' says Luci. 'What is "bonkers"?'

'Er, you know – loopy, barmy, completely doolally. As in mad as a hatter, only madder.'

'But I am not *mad*.' Luci flashes her dark eyes. 'I know it is not "bonkers" because I *saw* him.'

I look at Si, and expect to see him rolling his eyes. After all, it's ridiculous. But the way he looks back isn't exactly reassuring.

'Who knows, Daniel, what may lurk in the deep places of the world?'

'Right, that's it,' I say, snatching the skull candle from Luci's hand. 'I'm going down there. Because whatever it is that has you all spooked, it's certainly not Death. It's probably just a rat, or... er, two rats. Or something.'

For some reason, the kids don't sound reassured by this. But Luci silences them with her hand.

'Tell me the truth,' she says to me. ''ave you really seen Jojo as... as a...?'

'A ghost?' I say. And I nod. 'I'm sorry, Luci. Is there running water down there somewhere?' I point into the doorway.

'Oh, *mon dieu*!' Luci puts her hand to her mouth. 'The river! You mean... drowned?'

I want to comfort her, tell her it's all okay, but this whole thing's as far from okay as it's possible to be.

'I can still help him,' I say instead. 'There's a reason why he's still here. I can find out what it is,

79

and set him free. And put an end to all this Death malarkey while I'm at it.'

'No,' says Luci. 'No, if you go down there on your own, you will not come back. Even without Death, it is dangerous. I am going with you.'

There's a burst of protesting French from her housemates – mostly involving the word *non*, which even I can understand – but Luci ignores them. She takes a candle in a jam jar from the Sunglasses Kid, steps into the empty black doorway and turns back to look at me. She's scared, but her eyes are challenging me to follow.

Something tells me I'm in for a very different guided tour to the one Frenchy gave earlier.

I turn for a bit of moral support from Si, but he doesn't look back. He's gone very thin and faint and is clutching his wig in his hands. It looks like he's staring at something *behind* me.

I hate it when he does that.

'Si?' I say, my blood running cold at his expression. 'Come on, buddy, *you* know there's no such thing as Death, surely?'

'Mayhap, Daniel,' he says, his ectoplasm pooling on the floor beneath him like an embarrassing accident. 'Mayhap. And yet…'

He lifts his trembling hand and points over my shoulder.

'…how do you explain that?'

I revolve slowly. He's pointing not into the dark doorway but at the back of the cellar door. I follow his finger. There are deep slash marks in the wood, as if someone has attacked the door in a frenzy, attacked it with some kind of deadly metal implement. An axe perhaps, or a spade, or…

I swallow.

…a scythe?

I look down into the dark as Luci descends, and wish I had something a little less prehistoric than a skull candle to light the way. I glance back at the others. The Sunglasses Kid looks back at me and shakes his head. There's no confusion over what *that* means. I give them all my best here-goes-nothing look and pad down into the shadows after the girl.

The stairs go on for longer than I expected, and spiral slowly, so that by the time I turn to check behind me, the doorway is out of sight. When I reach the bottom Lucifane is waiting there. She's clearly terrified, but trying hard not to show it. Si, on the other hand, is a gibbering wreck.

'Daniel,' he dribbles, 'perhaps I should stay above and watch over the others…'

'Man up and pipe down,' I say. 'You're not wussing out on me this time.'

'But, Daniel, if Death himself is lurking below…'

'Come off it! You saw those slash marks on the door, Si. Nothing supernatural about those. But I'm going to need some paranormal backup either way. If only to deal with Jojo.'

'Are you really talking with the smoky man we saw upstairs?' comes Luci's quavery voice. The cellar of the house is cavernous around us, with a vaulted ceiling the candlelight hardly reaches. The cobwebs are big enough to catch a pterodactyl.

'Somebody's got to.' I shrug. 'So, Jojo – he was your boyfriend?'

Well, I'm only asking.

A mascara-loaded tear rolls down Luci's cheek and drops, leaving a perfect shadow of itself that even the best gothic makeup artist could never achieve.

'He was my brother.'

I wasn't expecting that. I'm just wondering what to say next when she steps closer.

'Dan?'

Eyebrow up.

'If you see him again, you will tell me, won't you?'

Eyebrow down. I nod.

Lucifane turns then and walks decidedly into the dark, toward the back of the cellar. There I see tower upon tower of crusty old wine racks, though I'm guessing it's years since anyone actually kept any Chateau Mouthwash down here. She stops beside one that is slightly out of place and puts her candle down. She heaves at it until the whole rack has swung back. Beyond is a gap in the brickwork like a scar in the wall.

'If you really want to understand,' says Lucifane, 'I will 'ave to show you everything.'

IO

THE CAVERNS OF BONE

I go through the gap in the wall first. Luci is so close behind me that we're leaning on each other for support as we pick our way down the narrow flight of steps. The candles aren't enough, so I ask Simon to turn his ghostlight up to max. He's still muttering things like 'the bowels of the earth!' and 'O, the infernal underworld!' but at least he's coming with me.

When we reach the bottom we have to duck through a tiny hole. And I see in an instant that we're back in the catacombs.

'You 'ave to know it is there,' says Luci, pointing at the nearly invisible hole behind us. 'This is why it is secret.'

'You mean the *cataflics* don't know about it?'

Luci holds up her candle and looks at me.

'So, you 'ave 'eard of them? I am impressed.'

So am I. I never remember things like that.

'The first to live in the squat,' she goes on, 'found this way in years ago. We 'ave used it ever since. Until...'

But she doesn't finish. Instead she creeps forward into the dark. I quickly catch her up.

'Luci, who owns the squat?' I've been wanting to ask this for ages. 'I mean, the actual building. Surely they're trying to get you out?'

'Some bank,' she says. 'In South America. The police brought letters from them for a while, telling us to get out. But we ignored them. They do not want anyone to live there, they 'ave boarded it up to keep as an investment. It is disgusting. These days Paris is just one big asset for bankers and businessmen.'

I say nothing. Politics is more Si's thing than mine. But I can't help wondering if these angry bankers, or whoever they are, might be doing more than just sending letters to the squat.

Then we reach a metal grill that blocks the way. I wonder what we'll do now, but I hear a squeak of rust and find that one of the bars just swings out. I climb through after Luci. When I look back through the bars I recognise where we are. It's the passageway I saw Jojo's ghost emerge from on my school visit.

Now we're walking through caverns I remember from earlier. It was all a bit spooky back then, but now, with nothing but candles and an ectoplasmic glow from Si, this place is pretty damn terrifying. Even for me.

Especially when the first skull looms out of the bone wall.

'Look, something 'as changed,' says Lucifane, pointing to the pile of spilt bones Baz and I knocked down earlier.

'Yeah?' I ask, as innocently as I can. 'Er... where are we going again?'

Luci heads off down a side passage and once again we are up against a wall of bars that blocks it. She squeezes between two that are slightly bent, and I do the same, almost losing a button from the coat.

'Now we 'ave left the public part of the catacombs,' says Luci. 'We must be careful how we step – it is less certain underfoot.'

We turn another corner and enter a long curving corridor, the walls of which are made up of more skulls than ever, in some kind of odd formation. And I swear they're watching us. There's a weird sound too, like a continuous echoing rustle. And that's when I notice that the skulls in the wall are in the form of giant, deathly letters.

'ET… IN…' I spell out as we go. 'ARCADIA… EGO? What does that mean? My French is, er… a little rusty.'

'It is not French,' says Lucifane. 'It is Latin.' And she shrugs.

'Si?' I say, looking at my sidekick. But if I'd hoped he'd be starting to pull himself together by now, I'm in for a disappointment. The sight of these words seems to have turned him into ghost jelly.

'It means, "Even in paradise, I am there,"' he quivers.

'Who's where? Come on, Si, quit dribbling and spit it out.'

'Death!' He turns to me. 'This phrase is used of Death. We must be gone from this place, Daniel! We are in the realm of the Great Destroyer himself, deep in the darkest depths of the earth, where nary a beam of the sun above can ever penetrate...'

But I'm off before I can hear any more of this tosh, because frankly, I'm getting a bit sick of all this. Hollywood would kill for an atmosphere like the one Si and Luci are creating, but I'm starting to smell something a bit fishy in all this. Like a herring, only redder.

As I approach the end of the passage, I finally recognize that weird babbling sound. It's running water, echoing back up the passageway. And then we're on the bank of a fast flowing and very pongy subterranean river.

It emerges from one slimy green brick archway and quickly vanishes into another. Two small boats have been dragged up one shore, secured with ropes. Spanning the river, forming the slightest of bridges to the passage beyond, are two lengths of chain, one at floor height, and another near my head.

Luci comes forward and stares down into the stinky flow. 'Jojo?'

'What were you doing on the other side?' I ask, hoping to take her mind off the watery fate of her brother. 'What's over the bridge?'

Luci says nothing. She hangs the candle jar around her neck, grabs the upper chain, and then shimmies across in one cat-like motion. I glance at Si, and he gives an elegant shrug. Well, what choice do I have? I shimmy across after her.

II

DANSE MACABRE

I find myself in a vaulted cavern, even darker than Baz's armpit. Then I start to see things.

At first it just looks like rubbish scattered about, but then I see that there are cushions down here. And some of the snack boxes aren't empty, and is that a dead plant I see, with burnt out incense sticks stuck in it? In the centre of the cavern something pale is looming, and I edge forward to scope it out. A thick, ornate stone pillar appears before me, about my shoulder height, carved with cavorting skeletons. And there's something on it.

It's an ancient CD player.

I put the candle beside it and glance round. Luci is in the shadows, using her candle to light others, bringing some sense of life to this dead place.

So this is where the *cataphiles* come to party. There's even a blood-coloured disco ball hanging above the pillar. It reflects the dancing light from the candles like a galaxy of red stars.

'I haven't been 'ere since it happened,' says Luci. 'We were dancing as usual. We were happy, celebrating. Then…'

'You saw the rat?'

'I saw *him*!' And Luci points down in the darkness beyond the pillar. 'I saw Death!'

I hold up the candle. Is that a further doorway, in a far wall?

I step forward but something gets caught up in my feet. It's a rolled-up newspaper.

I pick it up, and see that the date is just a few days before. It's a French newspaper, so that's about all I can understand. I'm about to drop it when something catches my eye, and my glasses nearly leap off my face when I see what it is.

It's a photograph of the Grim Reaper. Or rather, a still from some black-and-white film. And there's a story attached. Even I can pick out the word *catacombes* in the first sentence.

'Zooks, Daniel!' Simon gasps in my ear. He turns up his ghostlight and the article becomes easier to see. Though not, of course, easier to understand.

'Luci, what does this say?'

She takes the paper from me, screwing her eyes to read in the light of her candle.

'We are not the only ones. Other *cataphiles* 'ave seen him too, word 'as got out.' She looks up at me. 'A body 'as been found!'

'A body?' I say. 'You mean Jojo?'

'No, it is someone else, a man. There are many who find their way down 'ere. He was murdered, it says, and someone else is missing too. This is proof, Dan. Now even the press are talking about Death beneath the city. You 'ave to believe it.'

'Just because it's in a newspaper, doesn't make it real,' I say. Or rather snap, because I'm starting to get annoyed again. 'And how do they know he was murdered, this body they've found? It's pretty lethal strolling around down here. Maybe he just fell.'

Luci hands the paper back.

'He was killed,' she says, putting her hands on her hips and meeting my gaze, 'with a sharp metal blade. Like a curved sword.'

'Or a scythe!' Simon whispers.

I roll the newspaper up, slip it into my coat pocket and say nothing.

Then, and I'm not sure why, I reach up and press 'play' on the CD player. There's still a bit of oomph in the batteries and for a moment some of the cool sounds I heard the first night I was in the squat boom and jangle in the dark. The noise is a shock after our whispered conversation. Luci and Si both look appalled.

I'm about to switch it off and say something else when movement in the dark attracts my attention. There's someone there – a figure, emerging from the gloom, drifting above the ground. Trailing ectoplasm.

It's the ghost of Jojo.

I study him carefully. He's dripping with ghastly light as before but there's something a little more alert about him now, as if he's recovering his sense

of who and where he is. And one thing is certain –
he likes the music.

So I switch it off.

Deafening silence follows, and behind that the
babble of the underground river.

Jojo turns to me. He moves closer and closer, until
he's right in front of me. He has Luci's nose, I can't
help noticing.

'Daniel,' whispers Si. 'You must tell Lucifane.'

But I don't, not yet. Jojo looks like he wants to
speak himself, but he's making gasping sounds, like
he can't remember how to do it.

'Go on, mate,' I say, as encouraging as I can be
in the wrong language. 'Just tell me what happened.
What did you see?'

Jojo's ghostly face contorts with effort. He begins
to form a word.

'*C'ét…. C'était…*' he says, in a voice like wafting
silk that I can barely hear.

'He's here?' Luci cries, suddenly realizing and
rushing to me. 'Jojo?'

I hold up my hand, but it's too late – Jojo has
stopped trying to speak. He turns towards his sister,
and his face becomes anguished again. Lucifane
holds her hand out, groping in the air.

'Jojo?'

The ghost drifts towards her.

'Lucifane…'

He holds his hand out to hers, and I see her flinch as the cold of it hits her. I'm about to intervene when Jojo opens his arms and engulfs Luci in a spectral hug that would, I'm sure, make even a snowman seem cuddly. Lucifane gasps, but stays where she is.

'Jojo!' she cries out, and you can tell by her voice she's knows it's true. The candle falls from her hand and goes out in a tinkle of smashing jar.

Then, as quietly as he appeared, Jojo fades, the effort to communicate too much. In no time at all, he is gone, leaving nothing but a tumble of ectoplasm and a tearful smile on his sister's face.

'I think it's time to go,' I say.

'But we can't just leave him!'

'I think that's exactly what he wants,' I start to explain, but I stop when I see that she's crying. For a moment I wonder about putting my arm round her. In fact, I've pretty much decided to give it a go, when something happens to snap us both out of our thoughts.

There's a sound.

The sound of steps, coming from somewhere

beyond the altar, from the dark where the candle won't reach. And the steps are getting closer.

'Listen!' Luci grabs both my arms.

There's another sound now, a sort of scrunch POCK, scrunch POCK as someone makes their way on the gravel, tapping.

Tapping?

'I saw a documentary once, yeah? About how some rats can be really, really big…' I start to say, but give up.

'*C'est lui*…' Lucifane's voice is a hoarse whisper. 'It's him!'

'Si, quick!' I'm shouting now. 'Light it up!' I point into the dark where the sounds are.

Simon lifts a trembling hand and points, throwing his ectoplasmic glow down the chamber. I was right, there is a doorway there. And as I watch, a figure steps into that doorway.

He is swathed in billowing black, and his hood is deep. There is a curve of white metal above him. He steps into the room with the sound of scraping bone. Si gasps in terror as his light flickers and goes out.

But not before I see the face that looks out of that hood.

It's the face of a skull.

12

WHAT'S THE FRENCH FOR 'AAARGH!'?

Thinking back, I'm not quite sure how we got out of there. Simon vanished pretty instantaneously, so I don't suppose I ever had the chance to stand my ground anyway. Luci pulled me back, I do remember that, and somehow we both got across the chain over the river. And I remember

97

hearing the chain rattle furiously, just behind us, exactly as if someone big was coming across. But we were already running down the corridor, back past the skull letters.

ET IN ARCADIA EGO, eh? Well, maybe freaking so!

All I know for sure is we don't stop running till we're up the stairs and back in the squat. We fling the cellar door shut behind us, and Luci rams the bolt home. The others are all there, looking wild at our sudden appearance, and they start piling the rubbish back against the door in a frenzy of fear.

Then Luci puts her finger to her lips, and we all freeze. Everyone is listening. And after a moment, there's a sound. A rhythmic, throaty sound from the other side of the door.

Breathing.

Heavy, rattling breathing.

And the tap, tap, tap of bone on stone.

As we all stare in horror, the door handle turns.

We watch it slowly rotate till the latch disengages. The door presses inwards but the bolt and the clutter hold it, and the handle falls back. We look at each other, uncertain, then…

SLAM!

Something hits the door with enormous force. A point of metal is suddenly visible, flashing in the candlelight, splitting the wood. Then it vanishes as the blade – or whatever it is – is yanked out. A sound like slow, bony feet grows distant until, eventually, silence returns.

I turn and look at Luci, and find she's already staring right at me, white as angels.

I adjust the specs.

'Okay, maybe…' I say, still panting from the run, 'maybe it's not a rat.'

'But it's certainly *not* the Grim Reaper,' I say to Si.

We're sitting on the roof outside my room, and it's about one in the morning. Well, *I'm* sitting – Si is zooming around the tiny turret roof of my room, wringing his spectral hands and making the weather vane creak. We can't talk inside because of Brian, and we can't even think straight in the squat where terror has taken hold.

'But, Daniel, you saw it too.' Si stops his swooping long enough to wail in anguish. 'The scythe, the cloak, the empty pitiless eyes…'

'Stop flapping and listen, Si!'

He drifts down to eye level, round-eyed but almost containing his ectoplasmic distress. That'll have to do.

'Do you really think that Death, if he actually existed, would use a *real* scythe?' I say. 'And what was that noise we heard behind the door, before the blade hit?'

'The approach of the Destroyer, the sprightly tread of the Grim Harvester of Souls…'

'It was breathing. *Breathing*, Si! Since when have walking skeletons got out of breath? Since when do they have lungs? And since when has anyone been able to *outrun* Death?'

Si opens his mouth to wail some more, but then snaps it shut as my words sink in.

'Zooks, Daniel! You are right. But, mayhap…'

'Mayhap nothing. Think about it. These kids live in a squat, so they're trespassing, yeah? And Luci said the owner of the house wants them to leave. So don't you think there could be a slightly less supernatural explanation for all this?'

'Some manner of disguise?' I've got Si's interest now. 'You mean, a mortal man, masquerading as the Fourth Horseman of the Apocalypse?'

'Exactly.'

'But, Daniel, people have *died*. In the newspaper it said there have been murders. This goes far beyond Luci and her friends at the squirt.'

'That's all the more reason for us to do something about it. This isn't just a matter of helping Jojo move on, Si. I think we've got a nutter on our hands. A full-blown, suited-up psycho.'

Simon gives this some thought before speaking again.

'Of course, I suspected something of the kind all along…'

'Yeah, course you did.'

Simon puts his hands behind his back and averts his gaze. He seems to be back in freaky butler mode, but that's at least an improvement on the shrieking old maid impression he's been doing lately. I pull the newspaper from my pocket, and look at the article about Death again.

'Shame I can't read this. Si, make yourself useful for once and give me the gist again.' I hold the story up for him. And that's when I see it.

I lower the paper.

'Wait, I was just preparing the translation,' Simon says, but then he sees my face. 'Ah! You have discovered something yourself?'

I turn the paper round and hold it up again, this time showing him the back. It's the puzzle page. I tap on one part of the page in particular.

'A grid of lines? With numbers written within? Daniel, I do not see…'

'No, you wouldn't,' I say. 'But if you were a bit less behind the times, you'd know this was a sudoku puzzle. Don't ask me why, some people find numbers fun.' I roll the paper back up and pocket it again. 'And, where have we seen one of those being filled in recently?'

'The hostess of the Hotel Cafards?'

'Bingo. Hole in one. The receptionist does the sudoku. And she didn't sound too friendly towards her next door neighbours, did she?'

'But, Daniel, she is round and doughy, like an unbaked loaf. I cannot imagine she could dress up as the tall and ghastly figure we saw this night.'

I arch the eyebrow.

Si blinks at me for a moment. Then his eyes go big as cracked billiard balls when he gets it.

102

13

BREAKY AND THE BOGEYMAN

The porter doesn't see us behind the curtain, but we can see him as he stalks along the corridor. It's breakfast time the next day, the last full day of our school trip. The rest of the class are stuffing their faces with shrapnel toast and brown orange juice, but me, I'm on the prowl.

And as ever, Si is at my side.

'He is certainly tall enough, Daniel.'

'Too right,' I say, watching the porter turn a corner 'And look at that Frankenstein walk. He's our man, I reckon.'

'But how do you suppose he gains access to the catacombs? I hardly think he knocks on Lucifane's door and asks to borrow their secret tunnel.'

'Course not.' I dart out of hiding and pad down the corridor now the porter's out of sight. 'There must be a way in from the cellar of this place too.'

Si says nothing, but I can tell he's not convinced.

We reach the corner and peek round. There's only one flickery bulb and no window. There's also no sign of the porter, but at the end of the corridor is a door, and that door is ajar. And I can see steps going down.

'Okay, Si – time to get busy. Go and watch him.'

'To what end?'

'In case he does something that proves he's the nutcase who's running round the catacombs dressed as the Grim Reaper.'

'Is this really a useful employment of my talents?' Si sniffs. 'Watching a hotel porter count his onions?'

'Only one of us is invisible, remember? And it's not me. Now hurry up – I've got to check something too.'

Si drifts down the corridor on a wisp of offended ectoplasm, while I slip back upstairs. I'm on my way to Reception, to see if the newspaper the fat sudoku-loving receptionist reads is the same as the one I found in the catacombs. Oh, yes – I take this detective lark seriously.

Only, when I reach the lobby, something else stops me in my tracks.

Brian is sitting at a small corner table. He's scribbling furiously.

'Hi, Bri,' I say, hoping for a cheery response.

'Leave me alone.'

Okay.

Well, not *okay*, but understandable, I suppose.

'What's all that?' I ask, strolling over and eyeing the papers.

'Baz's homework. There's at least three months' worth.' Then he adds, bitterly, 'He was kind enough to bring it all with him.'

'But that's your fancy origami paper,' I point out. 'For your planes.'

'I won't be making any of those again, will I?'

He shoots me an accusing look. 'Not after what happened in the catacombs. Frenchy made that quite clear.'

I'm pretty narked off at this, and I'm about to tell Brian he shouldn't be such a doormat, but I stop myself. Baz is about twice his size, and Phelps is a tyrannical toad. There's really nothing Brian can do, is there?

I've let him down.

But at least I won't make it worse by giving him a lecture.

I walk over to the reception desk to collect my clue, but the fat woman isn't there. I glance around for a newspaper. There isn't one. There is, however, a cheap gossip magazine, open at the crossword. A *crossword*?

Of sudoku, there is no sign.

Crapsticks.

I wander into the dining room, feeling deflated.

'Ah, *bonjour*, Monsieur Dyer,' says Frenchy, his mouth full of cake. 'Finally crawled out of bed, then. Here.' And he gives me a doorstopper book of French comprehension and grammar exercises. 'Something for you to do while we're all eating ice-cream at the Eiffel Tower. Chapters 1 to 38, please. And I'll be testing you on it on the train home, so I suggest you get cracking.'

I slump down at a table, the book crashing onto the empty plate before me. I open the basket where the rock-like bread rolls are kept. There's only one left.

'Hur hur hur,' goes Baz from the table next to mine, as he tucks into an enormous plate of food. 'And when I've finished all this, I'll go and work off the calories by giving that little twerp Brian a good slapping, hur hur.'

The kids around him laugh along.

Then the girl called Tanya says something that catches my attention.

'Ooh, look, sir, it's the catacombs on the telly.'

We all look up at the blocky prehistoric television that teeters above us on a bracket. There is brown packing tape holding its speaker in.

'Well, this is interesting, class.' Frenchy squints up at the screen as he concentrates on translation. 'Apparently the catacombs have just been closed after a serious incident yesterday.'

Laughter, and lots of pointing at me.

'No, something even more serious than that,' Frenchy goes on. 'A French celebrity was exploring the catacombs last night – unofficially – when he came face to face with, was *attacked* by… hold on, I'm not sure I understood that…'

'What? *What?*' Everyone is goggling at Phelps now. He's not used to being the centre of genuine attention, and seems to be enjoying it.

'Well, they're saying he was attacked by Death. As in, the Grim Reaper. And according to what they're saying now, this isn't the first time someone has reported this in recent months, and… Good Lord, people are missing, and at least one body has been found! Apparently, there have been rumours for a long time, but the police are only just taking it seriously.'

On the screen now a crazed man in a pot-holing helmet is waving his arms and shouting about something. The interviewer can hardly get a word in. Then the screen is filled with the beaky nose of Commander Lavache.

His left eye is covered by a surgical patch.

There's a new round of laughter from my class, and a few cries of '*Brain* Cabbidge – what an idiot!'

Although Frenchy doesn't translate what he says, when Lavache speaks it's clear that he is a very unhappy man indeed. His good eye glares thunder and twitchy damnation out at us, before his face vanishes from the screen.

'Well, class,' Frenchy concludes, 'all I can say is, we're very lucky to have visited the catacombs yesterday, because they've just been closed down indefinitely. They are advising everyone to keep away from them. The official line is there's a murderer on the loose. But there are plenty who believe that Death himself really is haunting Paris.'

I tune out of the chatter that follows. All I'm thinking of is Luci and the fact that, even if the police close the catacombs, her cellar opens straight into them.

I'm just lifting the single remaining roll to my mouth – well, I've got to eat something, haven't I? – when Simon reappears from spying on the porter. I give him the eyebrow.

'Zooks!' he says. 'So much for your theory. All the man did was rip open a few bags of frozen bread rolls and pour them into baskets. I'm sorry to say he was picking his nose at the time.'

I lower my hand and put the roll back where I found it.

But then something catches my eye. I look at the grubby window and see the Sunglasses Kid peering in from the street outside. He spots me, and something about his fringe and chin tells me there have been developments. He points at the squat next door and vanishes.

I get up and walk out. In the lobby I almost lift Brian off of his chair.

'What are you doing?' he squeaks, making a grab for the homework. I knock it out of his hands.

'Leave it,' I say. 'Come on, we're going out for breakfast.'

14

I GET DECISIVE (SORT OF)

'What are we doing on the roof?'
'Trust me, Bri. And don't fall off.'

We drop down through the skylight of the squat. In the big room that's the heart of the place, the first thing I notice is that there's a huge flat-screen TV propped against the wall, obscuring the light from the stately windows. A bundle of cables snakes out

111

of one of those windows and head off to the hotel next door. On the screen is more news coverage of the story that Death himself is lurking beneath the pavements of Paris. In front of the screen sit the Goths and emo kids of the squat, passing round a carrier bag full of odd-shaped and reject croissants.

'Is it my imagination, or are there fewer than yesterday?' I ask Si.

'I believe you are right,' Simon says. 'And indeed, I cannot see Lucifane here.'

With a jolt I realise it's true. The Sunglasses Kid appears in the doorway behind me and slides over.

'Bri, this is the Sunglasses Kid. Sunglasses Kid, this is Bri.' The kid shrugs a greeting. Brian squeaks back. That's the formalities taken care of.

'Where's Luci?' I ask.

The kid snaps both index fingers at me like I'm the man with the question on everybody's lips. I throw out a shrug to ask what the answer might be, and get a double digit downward point in reply.

The cellar!

And now I'm running, taking those steps three at a time, and sliding down the banister on the last straight with a shriek of leather from the coat. And the cellar door is open.

And all the stuff that was urgently heaped against it last night has been pulled to one side.

I point into the dark doorway and raise the eyebrow at the kid. Well, I want to make *absolutely sure* before I go running down into the dark to where some psycho is lurking, don't I? But the kid nods.

'On her own?' I ask.

Snap – the finger says it all.

'Daniel, you cannot.' Simon is hopping from one foot to another. 'You don't know what's down there.'

'Cool it, Si – it's just the porter from the hotel.'

'Yesterday you thought it was a rat,' he says.

'Things have changed since then, Si. Luci's down there on her own. I'm going after her.'

'Um...' Brian has finally caught up with us. 'Does that go where I think it goes?'

'Stick with me, Bri, and you'll be fine,' I reply, adjusting the coat.

'You said that before.'

'Yeah, well, like I said – things have changed. And now a friend of mine is in danger.'

We reach the bottom of the rough stone steps. The Sunglasses Kid isn't with us – his shrug as he handed over a skull candle made it clear he wasn't the suicidal type. So it's just me and Bri and Si, and a whole world of shadow down in the caverns of bone.

'Turn up your ghostlight, Si – I can't see a thing.'

'Very well, Daniel. But this is madness. How will we ever find Lucifane in this place? We must go back.'

But before I can reply, I stub my toe on a lump of rock and my 'ooph!' of pain blows the candle skull out.

Darkness.

'Oh, great.'

Then, suddenly, light. Blazing at me.

'Wouldn't it be easier to use a torch?' says Bri, and I see he's got one on his keyring, which is just what I would have expected from him.

'Why didn't you say anything about that before?'

He doesn't reply. But at least he has the sense to hand me the torch.

The first thing I do is bend over and pick up the dropped skull. I break the candle off and place the skull neatly on a pile of stacked bone in the wall, dusting the top with my cuff.

Well, it is someone's head, after all.

Then we're off again, Brian almost clinging to me, and Si only as far ahead as he dares, shining his eerie glow into the shadows as we go.

In no time, we're back into the public part of the catacombs, and something makes me creep forward as quietly as I can, though creeping on gravel is pretty much impossible. And sure enough, after a succession of agonisingly loud *scrunch scrunch* noises, a grown-up male voice comes echoing over to us.

'C'est qui? Qui est là?'

We freeze, and I switch off the torch. There's more *scrunch scrunch*ing now, only this time it's not us. Two torch beams erupt into the cavern ahead of us, and there's more French. The only thing I can understand is that the people who own these voices are pretty rattled.

'It is the police,' whispers Si. 'Two who have been left to guard this entrance to the catacombs. They don't seem very keen to advance any further.'

'But they might,' I whisper back. 'Go and do something diverting.'

'Such as what?'

'Use your loaf, Si.'

'My loaf? But I have no loaf.'

'Crumbs, Si, do I have to think of everything? Make some spooky footsteps somewhere behind them.'

'Oh, very well.'

And he slides off, vanishing into the wall.

'I think I preferred it with Baz,' whimpers Brian, behind me. 'At least he doesn't take me to the spookiest place in the world and talk to someone who isn't there!'

'Just hold on to my coat, Bri, and get ready to run.'

There's a squeak which sounds vaguely affirmative, so I crouch down and prepare to sprint. And that's when Si's diversion kicks in. Literally.

There's a clear and very crisp footfall, somewhere far away, from behind the policemen. In the quiet, as they stop to listen, there's another and another. Then the police start shouting '*Arrêtez!*' and moving away. That's our cue. I dart out of the shadows, dare to switch the torch on for just a second, and then rush for the passageway Luci showed me last time we were here.

There's another shout, and at least one of the policemen turns his beam onto us as we run, but I won't slow down for that. I reach the metal grille that blocks the passage. Two of the bars are still slightly bent, and I manage to squeeze through. Brian is right behind me, and gets through just as the two policemen reach the head of the passage.

'*Arrêtez! Arrêtez-vous!*'

But I'm not arrêting for anyone, not now. We pelt down the skull-lined corridor like sprinters in the Goth Olympics, and dart down a side passage, and then another and another. From far behind, there's an echoing jangle of keys as the men wrestle with the gate in the grill. They get it open, and even crunch a little down the passage, but they must realise we could be long gone by now. The last we hear of them is their nervous voices as they radio in what they've seen, whatever that is. And with Brian hidden under the tail of my coat, they may be reporting a strange four-legged creature for all I know.

'That was mad!' pants Brian, emerging from the coat. 'Can we just find your friend now and get out of here?'

'You know, Bri,' I say, flicking the torch back on, 'I like that plan. Let's do that.'

15

STYX AND STONES

'Luci!' I whisper-shout at the bottom of my voice. 'Luci, where are you?'

'If we weren't so far into this infernal place, I'd suggest turning back,' wails Si. 'As it is, I cannot even remember the way. We are trapped, Daniel. Lost!'

I wish I could ignore him, but he's right – I can't remember the way either.

'Luci!'

'What's that noise?' says Brian

'It's me, trying to shout without making any noise,' I answer.

'No, that other noise. Listen.'

We go quiet. And yes, there is something. Tinny and echoey, all at once.

'Music?' I ask.

I turn the torch on Bri and he's nodding.

'It appears to be coming from there.' Si points, and lights the way with his index finger.

I know of only one place where we can find music down here.

'Come on!'

We run a little further and see the opening of another passage. The music is louder now, and there's another sound too, one I've been straining to hear for some time: running water.

We turn into the passage, but immediately I put up my hand for the others to stop. Far ahead, I see the faint ectoplasmic glow of a ghost, hovering in the air. And in that glow, someone is sitting huddled in a small paddle boat beneath the archway of the underground river. The portable CD player is in her lap.

Luci.

With the spirit of her brother watching over her.

'Wait for me here,' I whisper to Brian.

'What, on my own?!'

'Nah, Simon'll keep you company.' And ignoring Bri's squeaks of protest, I walk slowly forward.

'Luci?' I say as I get nearer.

She looks up.

'Dan?'

'Luci, you can't stay here. Let's go, yeah?'

'I cannot just leave Jojo. He is still here, I can sense him. Why is he still here, Dan, if he… if he really…?'

'He did,' I say firmly. The sooner she accepts what happened to him, the better.

I look over at the spirit of Jojo la Mouche. He looks back, and I can see he's starting to get it together, to accept what's happened to him too. He gives me a nod and gestures to his sister and I know exactly what he means.

'He's still here because of you,' I say. I take off my coat and drape it over her shoulders. Well, it's what you do in moments like this, isn't it? When there's a shivering girl?

Then I sit down next to her and tell her properly.

'He can't rest easy, he can't go on to the Hereafter while he thinks you're in danger. But you'll always be in danger down here while some madman is on the loose. The best thing you can do for Jojo is get back up to the squat and stay there till the police catch this nutter.'

'Nutter? What is "nutter"?'

'Psycho. Madman. Like a normal person, only insaner in the brainer.'

'You really think it is just a person dressed up? I almost hoped...'

'Trust me, Luci – I know it is. And I'm pretty sure I know who it is, too.'

And I tell her my idea that the owners of Hotel Cafards are trying to drive Luci and her friends out of the squat with this whole sick stunt.

'The *porteur*?' She looks doubtful. 'Are you sure?'

'Yup. Well, mostly sure. It sort of looks like it might be him, all things considered. I think. Um...'

'I do not care who it is.' Luci sets her head defiantly. 'I just want Jojo to be at peace. I cannot leave him here, Dan, all alone.'

All alone? I remember Brian and beckon him over from the shadows. Luci stands as he approaches, and brushes herself down. She looks good in the coat.

'Luci, this is the rest of the rescue party: Simon, who you met before but can't see because... well, we've been through all that... and this is Brian, expert in paper aircraft and, er, mathematics. You're in safe hands now.'

Luci says, '*Salut*,' to Bri and Bri manages to squeak back. He's goggling at her, and I'm not surprised – despite the circs, she's as stunning as ever. In a sad but Gothically beautiful sort of way, that is. I mean, she's the only person I've ever seen who looks good in run mascara. And as for her slightly upturned nose...

Concentrate, Dan, concentrate.

'Is it really true that the only way to help Jojo is for me to leave?' She sniffs.

I nod.

'Then let us go,' she says.

I glance at the ghost of Jojo and see that he's understood. His face seems to brighten and a spectral wind blows through him, drying away some of the wetness his drowning has left.

'You should say goodbye now.' I point to where Jojo's ghost is. 'When it happens, it can happen quite quickly.'

Luci sniffs again but keeps her chin up. She turns

to her brother and holds up her hand as she did before. He reaches out.

'Um, what's that noise?' says Brian, at entirely the wrong moment.

'You asked that one already,' I say. 'Music, then running water, then girl, remember? Get with the programme, Bri.'

'No, that other noise. Listen.'

I listen. And I hear it.

Scrunch POCK, scrunch POCK…

It's the sound of someone walking on gravel and tapping the base of a long pole. It's a sound we've heard before.

'Zooks, Daniel!' Si projects his ghost light down the corridor, away from the river – down the way we came. The sound gets louder and louder until…

…we see him.

Tall and hooded, he stands at the edge of our sight, robed in black and carrying a staff topped with a cruel steel blade. He stops and there's a moment of terrifying silence before…

POCK!

…he stamps his scythe on the ground and lifts his head. Beneath the shadow of the hood a mouth of

123

gleaming white teeth grins back at us, above a chin of yellowing bone.

'Across the river,' I somehow manage to say. 'Quick!'

'But we cannot.' Luci clutches my arm. 'The way through, beyond the party chamber, is blocked. The grilles have been locked by the police.'

'You mean…?'

'Yes. *He* is standing in the only way out!'

I look back at the figure of Death. He lifts his scythe.

Then he comes for us.

I give the nearest of the two boats a kick. It hits the water, and the rope in my hand almost cuts my fingers off as I brace myself against the pull of the water.

'Er, this is the bit where you get in!' I shout, when I see they are all just staring at me in astonishment. Luci recovers first and jumps into the boat, making it rock like crazy.

'This is insane!' squeaks Brian.

'No,' I correct him, '*that's* insane,' and I nod my head in the direction of the deathly figure sweeping down on us. Death lets out a bellow of echoing, inhuman rage, and strikes the wall of the passage in his passing, slicing through ancient bone and raising a torrent of sparks.

'Okay!' says Brian.

He jumps.

Then the ghosts are there too, waiting above the boat to follow as we are whooshed away into the unknown. But there's a problem. If I step forward to jump, the water will just pull the boat away at the same speed. And I don't need Jojo's ghost to remind me what could happen to yours truly if I land in this rushing black water.

'Daniel! Jump!' Si waves his wig at me, and the others call similar words.

The extra weight is pulling the rope through my hands now, but the sound of another scything cut reminds me that I'll be dead in a second or two anyway, so what have I got to lose? I look up and see that Death is upon me – his weapon is raised, he begins his swing…

With an echoing cry of 'Crapsticks!', I jump.

There's a sensation of speed and sharpness and a CLANG as metal strikes the arch of the tunnel. I get a face full of brick fragments and I can't see. I reach out and feel the edge of the boat, and grab it, just as my body hits the water. I fall back, shocked by the icy cold, but arms grab my clothes and somehow I don't slip under.

And so, like this – with me mostly not in the boat at all – we are taken by the current and swallowed whole by the clamouring darkness of the tunnel.

16

LIFEBOAT OR DEATHBOAT?

For a while everything is so mad that I don't know what's going on. The cold makes it hard to think straight, so I don't even try, I just hold on as the boat buffets and spins in the current. But eventually, with the world in my head still turning, I risk opening one eye and find that everything else has stopped, that we're out onto the calmer waters of some vast, subterranean lake.

And someone is pulling at me.

'Get in, Dan. It's wet in the water.'

I look up and see Brian's ferrety silhouette against the combined ghost glow of Simon and Jojo right behind him. And I can't argue with his powers of observation – it *is* wet in the water. I reach into the boat and haul myself in, Bri tugging at me with the power of a very small Jack Russell. Luci is sitting at the front with a long-bladed paddle, propelling us gently. The torch is propped beside her.

'Gngnk…' I manage to say from the freezing pool I've made at the bottom of the boat. 'W-w-where are we?'

'I do not know, I 'ave never been here,' Luci says, straining to see ahead. 'But the only thing that matters is we 'ave escaped Death.' Then she turns and gives me a look that would stop a charging rhino and make it blush. 'Thanks to you.'

I sit up and shake the hair. A small white fish falls out and lands in my lap. It looks up at me with bulbous, unseeing eyes before springing into the air and plopping over the side.

'C...cool.' I pick up the coat from where Luci has dropped it, and slip it on. 'S...Si, any great ideas in that leaky head of yours?'

'For regaining the surface, you mean?' Si puffs ectoplasm from his bullet hole. 'To escape the hellish confines of this nightmare deep? To feel, once more, the golden touch of the eternal sun?'

'Yeah.'

'Then no. But something of practical importance has occurred to me, Daniel, especially given the sounds emanating from behind us.'

Emanating? What sounds are emanating? I turn back but I can't see a thing beyond the spectral glow in the boat – the lake must be enormous. But I can hear rushing water behind. And...

'Luci, stop paddling a moment. Bri, quit fidgeting. Listen!'

From behind, barely audible above the constant roar of the fast water that feeds the lake, there's a steady *swoosh sploosh* sound.

'Si?'

'Well, while we're all celebrating our escape from the clutches of Death,' my oh-so-helpful sidekick says, 'it might be well to remember that there was a *second* boat.'

129

I look at Luci and she looks back. No one looks at Brian, but we both know what he's thinking from the frightened squeaks that break out.

I pick up the torch and shine its puny light into the dark behind. It's not enough to give more than the barest impression of what's there, but then again, it's surprising how little light you need to spot the Grim Reaper as he stands in a boat, propelling himself along with great sweeps of his scythe.

'Dan,' says Luci, in a trembly voice. 'What is that word you always say, when things are going badly?'

'Er... crapsticks?' I suggest.

'*Oui*. That is it.'

'Let's take it as said, then, shall we? And row!'

Luci jumps forward again, and starts paddling like an Amazon warrior. There's a big pole in the bottom of the boat, and I grab that, shoving it in the water behind us, trying to propel us along the bottom of the lake.

Only there is no bottom to this lake. At least, none I can find.

'Bri, use your hands,' I say. 'Si, any chance you can blast us along with ghost power?'

'Alas, no,' he says with a look of elegant regret,

as Brian's small splashes join our own efforts. 'But I suggest you increase speed somehow. See, he gains on us!'

I look round and sure enough, it turns out that a scythe is an excellent paddle. And maybe Death sees me looking, I don't know, but at this moment a horrible, ringing laugh breaks out. It booms round the lake and the invisible cavern above.

'Okay, Si – that's not the hotel porter, is it?'

'I fear not.'

'And the owners of the squat or South American bankers or whatever? It's not likely to be them either?'

'Why would anyone wanting to drive out Luci and her friends terrorise the *whole* catacombs, Daniel?'

'But, surely you don't think…?'

'He comes with a strength and vigour that is scarcely human, his face is a mask of bone…'

'But, Si, *you're* dead. And you didn't see the Grim Reaper when you copped it, did you?'

'Well, no, but I did have a bullet expanding in my brain at the time. Perhaps I missed him.'

'I can see something,' Luci calls. 'Up ahead. It is another tunnel, another way out!'

I strain forward, and sure enough, there's a vast stone arch looming in the darkness ahead, below a bloom of sparkling stalactites that hang from the rock above.

I turn the pole in the water behind us, and force the front of the boat that way. With Luci still paddling we should be able to reach the arch before our deathly pursuer. And maybe that explains what happens next.

'What's that noise?' says Brian

'Bri, will you stop hearing noises!'

'No, listen – it's like…'

But then the world explodes with a sound louder than any I could have imagined. A patch of inky water beside the boat flies into the air and sprays over us.

'… a gun being cocked,' Brian finishes weakly.

And it's true. In the boat behind us, Death has thrown down his scythe and is taking aim with a very un-supernatural – but all the more deadly for that – shotgun.

'Get down!' I shout, wondering how much protection the sides of this little boat will give. And I find out immediately as a second boom nearly bursts my eardrums. A chunk of boat vanishes from the woodwork right beside my head, carrying my purple specs away with it.

'Double barrelled,' I gasp, peering back through the hole. 'Only two shots. He's re-loading!'

'Then we 'ave no time to waste,' cries Luci, and she stands behind me. Before I can say or do anything, she takes up the paddle, swings it through 180 degrees of pure wronged-Goth anger, and lets go.

I've never seen a paddle look more like a weapon of vengeance in my life, but that's exactly how it appears as it swirls through the air. It hits Death square in the chest with a satisfying *thud*, knocking him off his feet. There's a *ploof* as the shotgun spins into the water. Then Luci follows through with a torrent of filthy-sounding French that even I'm glad I can't understand.

The ghost of Jojo lets out a whoop of spectral glee and dances crazily around his sister. She has never looked more like a panther than she does now.

'One small problem,' Si points out, in his most infuriating voice.

I give him the eyebrow as I stand beside Luci.

'We needed that paddle to move.'

We look back at the other boat and see Death stagger to his feet. The bony grin from the hood suggests that he's realised the same thing. He picks up his scythe, letting out another peal of terrible laughter. With a great dig of the scythe into the water, he surges towards us.

'Crapsteeks!' says Luci.

17

THE LIGHT AT THE END OF THE TUNNEL

I grab the pole, and begin pushing for all I'm worth. And amazingly I can finally touch the bottom, so we ease forward in our desperate, slow-speed boat chase. But I'm not entirely concentrating on our predicament, not right now, because I've just noticed something.

I saw it as Death got back to his feet. But it's only now that I realise what it is.

'If only I 'ad something else to throw!' Luci cries in exasperation, as she looks about the interior of the boat with the torch. 'But there is nothing!'

But she's wrong. There *is* something we could throw. And what starts as an idea that her words bring into my head quickly becomes a notion that links everything together. And that becomes a plan.

'Bri, have you got any paperclips in your pocket?'

'Er…'

'It's not a trick question, Bri!'

'Er…' He rummages in his jeans. 'Yes, a few, but…'

I drop the newspaper – the one I found in the catacombs last time and which is still rolled up dry in my coat pocket – on his lap.

'Make a plane, Brian. Make the best paper aeroplane of your life.'

'But…'

'Dan?' Luci looks at me like she can't believe what I'm saying.

'Oi, can't I get a little trust around here? I'm the expert on the scene, yeah? The kid who sees dead people? And I'm telling you, Brian, to make like a sheep and *fold*!'

Brian squeaks, but as I dig the pole again and again into the water, I hear him tear off a sheet and start his furtive rustlings. I'm about to say something to hurry him along, when he beats me to it.

'It's more of a dart than a true plane,' he explains, fixing a paperclip on the nose and holding it up. My mouth falls open. It's so astonishingly, blindingly complex that I can hardly believe he's made it so fast. 'I added a fifth stabiliser along the spine, so that – '

'We'll look at the graphs later!' I shout. 'Just chuck it at old bony face!'

'What?' say both Brian and Luci.

Death lets out another peal of inhuman laughter as he gains further. He's going to catch us. He waves his scythe in triumph.

'Brian! Throw the freakin' plane!'

Bri gives me a wild look, but then turns in the boat anyway, getting ready to throw. I lean over to Si and whisper a quick instruction in his spectral ear.

Brian throws his plane.

And for someone who can make paper do foldy things I didn't think possible, it turns out Brian's pretty rubbish at the actual throwing part. In fact, by the time Si manages to catch hold of it with his mind, the plane is almost in the water. But using the same telekinetic power that made Baz's jeans fall down on the train, Si sweeps Brian's plane high up into the air.

'Crikey!' says Brian.

As we all watch, the plane zooms around the cavern at the very limit of sight, gaining speed as it goes. Even Death stops to look up, his hood falling back. What a shame only I can see Simon flying it in a blaze of spectacular ectoplasm. He takes the plane up in a glorious loop into the darkness above. When it reappears, it rockets downwards like a bolt from on high, straight at Death.

And into his right eye socket.

Death lets out a very human sound – 'Aiii!' – and falls in a billow of black cloak and flailing arms.

This time he doesn't get up. We can all hear the moaning from the bottom of his boat. I look at Brian. His eyes are wide with astonishment.

'Something tells me that really will be the greatest plane of your life, Bri.'

He stares up at me.

'I...' he starts. Then his face changes. 'I... I can hear something.'

'Freakin' hell, Brian!'

'No, so can I,' says Luci. 'What is that?'

And there *is* a sound, a sound that's growing around us – a murmur that's becoming a roar. Then there's a glow, which flickers in the tunnel ahead, before turning into a torrent of light, making us all hold up our hands to our eyes.

A motor boat burst from the tunnel and speeds right past, spraying us with water and setting our little craft rocking like crazy.

'*Arrêtez-vous!*' comes a cry from the dark, amplified through a megaphone.

It's the boys in *bleu*.

The police vessel turns sharply and slows, making ready to head back to us. But, by chance, this brings it right alongside the second boat. Where – in the blaze of the police spotlight – a figure in black sits up, his face a mask of death. And that mask is ripped off, as the person wearing it clutches at his right eye.

His left eye is already covered with a surgical eye patch.

The engine of the police boat cuts immediately.

'But Daniel!' Si is at my side in a moment. 'Who is that?'

'*Le Commandant* Lavache!' Luci gasps. 'But… but he is the 'ead of the *cataflics*. *He* is doing this?'

I adjust the coat. If I still had my specs, I'd correct them too.

'Yeah, the guardian of the Empire of the Dead,' I say. 'Spent so much time down here, he's gone native, I reckon. Fancied the job of Emperor himself.'

'But how did you know?' Si is swirling around me impatiently. '*How* did you know who it was?'

'When Luci knocked him down, I saw straight away it was someone in a mask. And someone I'd seen before too. Think about it, Si. What's the one thing you can't hide when you wear a skull mask? Your hooter. Especially when it looks like the front of a battleship. His nose stuck right out through the hole in the middle of the skull, all shiny with sweat.'

By now I'm punting us over to the police. Well, they're our ticket out of this place, aren't they? But I'm in no hurry. Besides, right now they're too busy being flabbergasted by the fact that their chief is the murdering psycho behind all the madness that's been going on down here recently to pay much attention to us.

Yet.

Jojo's ghost makes a triumphant loop around his sister and his spectral glow becomes golden. I recognise the signs.

'Luci, now it really is time to say goodbye to Jojo.'

He's all around her and I'm about to point this out, but I can see from her face that she knows he's there. Maybe she can't see dead people, but she's not without something of that gift.

She closes her eyes for a moment. When she opens them again she is looking right at me.

'Thank you, Dan. *Merci!* Jojo is at peace now. I can feel it. And it's all down to you.'

I give my best shrug, one the Sunglasses Kid would be proud of.

'There's just one little thing before he goes, though,' I say. I hate this part, but I am in business, after all. 'Sorry we didn't get the chance to go over the small print before, but there is a tiny favour Jojo could do for me. Before he goes over to the Hereafter, that is. Let's call it… my fee.'

Luci looks confused. I give her my best lopsided grin and explain.

She looks even more confused for a moment, but then she smiles – smiles brilliantly. And with the sun of that smile through the rain of her tears, her face is a rainbow of emotion. She steps over to me and nods, pushing a strand of loose hair from her face. I go a bit wobbly in the knee department, but manage to stay upright as her kiss lands on my lips.

And it is the exact polar opposite of crapsticks.

Is there a word for that? Not that I care. It's my entire trip to Paris and everything that's happened to me there, all rolled into one ear-tingling moment.

Then I have an overwhelming sense of Jojo being there too, just for a second. I go cold as he passes through me. By the time I open my eyes, he has gone.

Though not entirely.

As Luci steps back and gives me a shy glance, I know that one small part of her brother will remain on earth a while yet. And I have the chance to test that part straight away.

As the police pull their disgraced commander from his boat and slap the handcuffs on, he stops whimpering for a moment, turns his blind eyes up to his former colleagues and cries:

'*J'aurais pu réussir mon coup si ces gamins ne s'en étaient pas mêlé!*'

And I understand perfectly.

18

THE BOY WHO
CHEATED DEATH

Well, we're soon being towed out through the tunnel and away. The police don't really know how to handle us so we just stay in our boat and try to look innocent. Not easy when one of us is wearing a death's head coat and the other looks like she's about to audition for a Goth-rock musical about

143

teenage vampires. But I don't care. Luci's holding my hand, and I just sit there feeling fuzzy.

There's quite a reception at the end though. It's clear the police have radioed through with the astonishing news about Lavache – there's a whole crowd of uniforms waiting to clap him in irons. We're not exactly treated warmly either, but hey, I'm used to that. There's talk of having to make a statement and vague threats about trespass charges, but all that evaporates when we finally reach the surface and emerge into the daylight.

It seems the whole of Paris is waiting for us.

'How did they hear about it?' I wonder aloud, staring at the enormous crowd.

'Mayhap through the pocket speaking boxes the policemen are carrying,' says Si, in his old-fashioned way.

But however it happened, the press are waiting outside in a scrum of cameras and microphones. When Lavache is led out, still in his deathly robes, and with a young policeman following, carrying his scythe and skull mask, the world goes crazy with questions and flashbulbs.

'Blimey, Si, look,' I say. 'There's Frenchy and the others. We must've been reported missing

144

or something. Phelps won't be too pleased about that.'

'Keep close to young Brian, Daniel. I see that thug Baz there too.'

And that's when another idea occurs to me. Hey, it's all go in the brain box today. Besides, the cries for information from the Press reach a fever pitch, and it would be impolite not to give it to them, wouldn't it? I jump onto the roof of a nearby police car, and drag an astonished Brian up beside me. Before the coppers can object, I raise my hands for silence. And I get it.

Then I start to speak.

It feels odd, talking in the fluent French that Jojo gave me in return for helping his sister. Like someone else's mind is supplying the words that my own wants to say. And in a way, that's exactly how it is.

First I tell the press about my outcast friends in the squat. I don't give any names, but draw a vivid verbal pic of their need to put a roof over their heads in the face of intolerance, broken homes and absent overseas landlords. Someone in the crowd shouts, '*Vive la France!*'

Then I mention the catacombs, and the partying and how no one can blame a bunch of likeable misfits for making the most of the caverns beneath their feet, can they? Well, can they? When I get onto the appearance of Death himself in the catacombs and the sad fate of poor Jojo, you could hear a baguette drop. And that's when I push Brian forward.

He's the real hero, I declare. I tell of Brian's bravery in deciding that something should be done to help the terrified young people in the squat. I wave my fist in the air when I explain how Brian single-handedly deduced who was behind the attacks and hatched the plan to stop him. I gush with gratitude at his generosity in letting me come along too.

When I get to the bit where Brian not only rescued the girl, but defeated Death with one of his amazing paper aeroplanes, there's a gasp of such utter disbelief that I wonder if I'm overdoing it a bit. Fortunately, that very plane – preserved as Exhibit A in the hands of a wide-eyed policewoman – is held aloft on cue.

The clicking of cameras is almost deafening then.

I raise Brian's hand and declare, in rousing French, that he is nothing less than the boy who cheated Death; the hero of the Paris underworld. Then I hop down, leaving him blinking in a renewed storm of photography.

Brian is every inch the terrified squirrel as he faces the crowd. Obviously he knows I'm lying, but I doubt anyone will listen to him now anyway. Once people get hold of a good story, the truth is the first thing to get trampled in the stampede. And there's a mighty rush of people now. Brian finds himself hoisted into the air, his squeaks of protest ignored. Then the cheering starts.

'That was very generous, Daniel,' says Si, puffing his approval in little white clouds of ectoplasm.

'Yeah, well, he needed a break,' I reply, looking over to my classmates.

Baz is at the front, a look of leaden anger on his meaty mug, but he soon vanishes behind the others as they jostle with reporters to get near Brian, to share in his sudden celebrity. The girl called Tanya shouts 'Juh swee don le meme class as him!' as she grabs Brian's sleeve and holds on. 'Juh swee his girlfriend!'

Another storm of cameras.

'I reckon he's pretty bully-proof now, don't you, Si?' I say. 'Besides, it's not good for business if *I'm* in the spotlight, is it?'

'Indeed not, Daniel,' my ghostly sidekick replies. 'But there is one light you cannot escape so easily. Look over there.'

I look over there. Luci has slipped to the edge of the crowd, easily distancing herself from the overwhelmed police. But she's got her eyes turned up to max and she's aiming them right at me.

I manage a not very cool wave, and wonder if I'll ever find my inner James Bond.

Luci blows me a kiss. And I swear I can actually feel when it lands like an incoming missile.

Then she's gone, vanishing into the urban shadow of a Paris side street.

I wish I had my purple specs right now.

'All in all, a very satisfying outcome, Master Dyer,' says Si then. 'You not only rescued Jojo but you even managed to deal with your class bully in a most intelligent way.'

'Eh?'

'Oh, yes. When one cannot defeat one's enemy by force, one acts to make him so irrelevant that he does not need defeating at all. You are learning, Daniel. You know, for a while I honestly thought you were going to try to *fight* him. With your fists!'

'Yeah,' I say, staring at my shoes. 'Yeah, it's just as well I didn't try that, isn't it?'

And I stroll back to join the rest of my class. Frenchy is standing there, his mouth opening and closing like a goldfish who doesn't get that the fly's on the other side of the glass.

'How…?' he splutters. 'How did you…?'

'*Réussi à apprendre la langue française en quelques jours?*' I suggest, finishing his question for him. He nods in a twitchy, slightly mad way. Yes, it seems he really would like to know how I managed to learn French so fast. I look back at him. Then I give him my biggest, most Gallic shrug.

I think that says it all, don't you?

And by the time we're allowed back on the bus, Frenchy even manages to smile in my direction. I must remember to give him his grammar book back tomorrow.

As we take our seats once again in the flea-bitten bus – ready to be whisked back to the delights of the Hotel Cafards – Baz makes one last attempt to get at Brian. But it's hopeless – he's drowned out by the sea of kids. They deposit their new hero in the middle of the back seat, and cluster round. The girl called Tanya snuggles beside him, tearing pages out of a guide book of Paris and handing them round. Everyone wants to know how to make the plane that defeated Death, it seems. Brian's going to have a late night tonight. And somehow I just know Baz'll be making planes too, before the end of it.

And me? Well, I settle back into the leatherette and school bus fluff all on my own, and recede into the coat. Well, not *all* on my own, obviously. Simon is at my side, with a snaggletooth grin of spectral pride I'm glad only I can see.

But there are no prizes for guessing who I'm thinking about.

This is my last night in Paris. Tomorrow I have to say goodbye to Lucifane.

19

LAST MANGO IN PARIS

I hardly sleep that night. And not just because of the sound of music and partying that comes from one of the rooms below as our class celebrates their last night away and Brian's awesomeness. It's a party they somehow forgot to invite me to. I sleep a bit though, I must do, because when I open my eyes next

I see that Bri is lying on top of his bed, a huge smile on his face. Like the squirrel who got the acorn.

I'm pleased for him.

It's dark outside, but my watch says it won't be for long, so I get up and pull on the coat. The corners are still a bit damp from wearing it over wet clothes, but I'm glad of it as I slip out through the window and into the predawn cold of a Paris morning.

I half expect to see her on the roof next door, but why should I? I must be going soft in the head.

'Daniel?'

Simon is suddenly at my side, all ectoplasm and spectral concern.

'Back to London today, Si. And all that.'

'Indeed. But Paris isn't so far. Certainly, it's closer now than it ever was in my time. Though there's no place like home, as they say.'

'Yeah, they do,' I agree. But I'm thinking of something Luci said the first time I visited the squat, about how she and her friends had turned an empty building into a home – a home for those who don't fit in anywhere else.

I jump across and stroll over to the skylight. I've got the coat, I've got Si, I've got my pale and interesting looks – it's everything I need to start again in a new city, isn't it? Well, isn't it?

I slide down the ladder.

The house is silent.

So silent that I know immediately it's empty.

I crouch in the dark, straining my ears anyway. The sound of a distant police siren drifts in from far away. I stand and walk slowly down to the big room.

'It's quite a mess,' says Si, swooping about. 'It looks like they left in a hurry. But why? The Deathly stalker of the catacombs had been defeated, there was nothing more for them to fear. Why did they leave?'

I shrug – a small, British one this time.

I know why they've gone. Luci and her friends live below the radar, off the map. Under the ground. The press were bound to find them sooner or later, hungry for more of the story I span last night. They could never live with that. After all I'd done to protect it, the squat was over anyway.

But there's something I see – a glint in the ghostlight from Si.

It's a pair of purple shades, on the arm of the big fancy chair.

I slip them on.

'Daniel,' says Si, at my side, 'there's nothing else for you here. Let us return to your home and your family. You will have other clients. The one thing the world is never short of is ghosts and their regrets.'

'Yeah. But I think I'll just take one last look at the catacombs, Si. You know, to see what I could have won.'

The cellar door is slightly open. I look around for a skull candle, but I don't see one. In fact, all the bones that once decorated the squat have vanished completely. There is a candle in a jam jar, though, and a small box of matches.

I light up and walk down.

Nothing here has changed of course. The corridors of bone, the macabre sculptures – all as creepy as before. I walk through the public areas I now know so well, half expecting to be stopped by a policeman, but there's no one at all. I squeeze between the bars as if they aren't there.

There are no boats beside the river when I reach it, but there wouldn't be, would there? I shimmy across the chain and creep into the party chamber. I'm sorry that I never got to see this place in full swing. I could tell Si that ghosts aren't the only ones with regrets, but I can't be bothered.

The chamber is almost unrecognisable. It has been cleaned entirely – the snack boxes, litter, candles and cushions are all gone. Even the huge glitter ball has been taken down. And something else is different too.

'They put them all back,' says Si, sweeping his light across the walls of bone. 'All of them.'

And he's right. All the skulls from the squat have been fixed back into the wall of the Party Cavern. But not just any old how. They have been arranged in giant letters, letters that spell out two words:

AU REVOIR.

Till we meet again.

And whether that's a message to me or to this place or to Death himself, I guess I'll never know.

But hey, that's my life all over.

And I never let it get me down.

W hat's that? You want to know what Lavache said as he was arrested? You want it *translated*?

'It's only fair to your readers, Daniel. We don't all have the chance to borrow languages from ghosts.'

You understand it, though, don't you, Si?

'Naturally. He believed he "would have got away with it, too, if it hadn't been for you... er... interfering children".'

Close enough, Si. That's close enough.

Dan's first adventure is also available from Bloomsbury.

When Dan's spectral sidekick Simon brings him the spirit of a teenage shoplifter, things get seriously out of control. Now Dan's on the hit list of a very dangerous and very badly dressed gangster – not to mention being stalked by a crazed Victorian magician who cut off his own head. (Don't ask.)

£5.99   9781408154120